# TO THE FAR SIDE
# OF THE FOREST

# TO THE FAR SIDE
# OF THE FOREST

## E. ROSE SABIN

**Arucadi Enterprises, LLC**
St. Petersburg, Florida
2015

ISBN: **0692535071**

ISBN-13: **978-0692535073 (Arucadi Enterprises)**

For my dear young cousins,
Teddy and Mary

# 1

# CEREMONY

"Serollyn, if you don't hold still, I'll never finish brushing the snarls out of your hair."

"I'm sorry, Grandmother. I'm just so excited."

"Of course you are, child." Grandmother Sudy wielded the brush with a vigor that brought tears to Serollyn's eyes. "And the sooner you're ready and out of this house, the sooner the ceremony can take place."

Grandmother was right; she was acting like a child, but Serollyn could not sit still. She was too eager to meet the clan council and receive the councillors' blessing and the materials for the ritual that would let her join her agemates in being welcomed into adulthood. She'd rehearsed that ritual so often: drawing the circle, speaking the words to the Life Lenders, making obeisance, and finally meeting her very own life-guide.

What would the life-guide be? A white tern like her mother's guide had been? A dove like Laki's? A gazelle like the piper's? Surely not a great-cat like Marleon's.

Whatever came to her she would treasure. It would become the closest of companions, known only by her, seen and heard only by her, a lifelong friend, advisor, and confidant. She couldn't wait to return with her guide and to hear the council declare her a full member of the clan, with all the privileges and responsibilities attendant on adulthood. The last of her age group to go through the ceremony, she was more than ready to rejoin her age-mates as an equal.

"Serollyn!"

"Sorry, Grandmother." At her grandmother's rebuke she tried again to hold her body still, but all her insides were shaking.

"There." Her grandmother put down the brush at last and swung Serollyn around to face her. "Your hair shines like polished obsidian." She spread the long straight hair out so that it draped over Serollyn's shoulders like a shawl. "You look very like your mother, you know. She was a beauty such as you are becoming."

"I barely remember her," Sudy said. "I wish she were here on this special day."

"So do I, Serollyn, so do I. On this day and every day."

Suddenly sad, Serollyn asked, "Do you think she could be alive somewhere? Hunters found no trace of her. But she'd have come back to us if she could've, wouldn't she?"

"I'd think so. She took your father's death so hard … But this is not the time to think sad thoughts." Sudy picked up the brush and, although she had declared the grooming complete, she brushed furiously for several seconds before putting the brush down again and leaning forward to give Serollyn a kiss on the cheek. "Think of nothing more now but the Life Lenders and the gift of a life-guide," she counseled.

"I will, Grandmother. And when I have one, maybe my life-guide will help me find my mother, or at least find out what happened to her."

"Don't think that far ahead," her grandmother cautioned, smoothing her hand over Serollyn's hair.

"This is the last time I'll wear my hair loose like this," Serollyn mused. "After today I'll be wearing it in the braid that shows I have a life-guide."

Grandmother Sudy closed her eyes and whispered, "May it be so."

"It will, Grandmother, and thank you. May I go now?" Serollyn stood and adjusted her best wraparound, of a glossy red cloth with a design of yellow hibiscus. She smoothed it carefully over her budding breasts and headed for the door.

"Wait a moment, child," her grandmother said. "Take deep breaths and calm yourself. You're too eager. Heed my warning. The ritual does not force a life-guide to come. The guide will come or it won't."

Serollyn laughed. "Grandmother, you're being silly. The life-guides always come. Everyone has one."

"Not everyone."

"You mean Kreia?" Serollyn grew quiet again, thinking of the girl who had given herself to the Death Stealers by throwing herself over the bluff onto the rocks below when her life-guide failed to come.

"Kreia, yes, and others, too."

"What others?" Serollyn's eyes widened. "I don't know about any others. Did they die too?"

"No, only Kreia died, and I don't want you to think about her." Sudy joined her at the door and kissed her cheek. "Go on, now. The council will be waiting."

Serollyn ran from the house, in too great a hurry to ponder her grandmother's puzzling words.

Such a long run. From the house she shared with her

grandmother, on the edge of the village, near the forest, to the Great Hall in the village center where the council would be assembled under the high roof. She wouldn't have slowed had it not been for the urgent call from the shadows of a clump of nerga trees.

"Pssst, Serollyn! Over here!"

She slowed. Her friend Vali stepped out of the shadows, waved frantically, and then retreated into the protection of the trees.

Annoyed, Serollyn jogged to the clump of trees. "What's the matter?" she asked. "The council is waiting for me."

"I know," Vali spoke barely above a whisper. "There's something I need to tell you before you go."

"Hurry up, then. I don't want to be late."

"Well, Marleon and I, we want everything to go well for you, and, well, we're sure it will and you'll get your life-guide." Vali stopped and reached out to quickly clasp Serollyn's hand. Serollyn felt Vali's hand shake in the seconds before her friend jerked her hand away and stepped back into the shadows.

Serollyn was too impatient to be curious about her friend's odd behavior. Whatever the problem was, it could wait until after she returned. She'd be better equipped to deal with it once she had her life-guide.

As resumed running she called back to the retreating Vali, "Tell Marleon I appreciate his good wishes—and yours."

"But I need to warn you—," Vali called after her.

Late already, Serollyn kept going.

She skidded to a halt in front of the great hall and took deep breaths until she could enter at a more dignified pace.

Feeling all jiggly inside, she walked through the wide front entrance.

All the councillors were assembled, and several frowned at her late arrival. The clan mother held out a hand to her and drew her into the center of the room, then stood with her as the other councillors formed a circle about them.

"You have not broken fast this morning?" the clan mother asked.

"I have not," Serollyn said, her voice betraying her nervousness with a quaver she could not control.

"You have cleansed yourself thoroughly?"

"Yes."

"You have meditated as required?"

"For more than the required time." Her voice grew stronger with each assurance.

"You have prayed to the Life-Lenders to grant you a guide?"

"I have, Clan Mother, with all my heart," Serollyn avowed truthfully.

The clan mother nodded and smiled. "We will add our prayers to yours."

The councillors joined hands, and the clan mother intoned: "O you who lend us our lives, we beg you to grant our petition and send to this daughter of the clan the guide selected to show her the paths she is to walk through life."

"May it be so," the councillors chanted.

Serollyn repeated, "May it be so."

Without another word the clan mother placed into her hands a cloth-wrapped bundle, the councillors broke their circle and formed two lines. which Serollyn walked between to reach the door. Each councillor touched her shoulder as she passed, and each touch sent chills of excitement coursing through her body.

Clutching the bundle, resisting the urge to run, Serollyn marched through the village, staring straight ahead. Nothing must distract her on this most important walk to the high cliffs overlooking the sea. She paused at the edge of the village. Was that Vali peering out from the shadows of those mango trees? She did not turn her head. If it was Vali, she should not be there. Her friend knew that after leaving the Great Hall, Serollyn could not speak to anyone until the ritual was done. It was a violation of clan law to approach or be seen by a candidate who had been blessed and was en route to the place of ritual.

On the cliff overlooking the sea, Serollyn opened the bundle and spread out the cloth. On it she placed the contents: a hunting knife, a fishhook, a sharpened rod for planting seeds, and a needle, representing the most common ways of serving the clan, and most precious of all, the long red ribbon to be bound into the braid in which she would wear her hair to signify her acceptance as an adult clan member. When her life-guide came, she would gather her hair into that long single braid before reporting back to the council.

After carefully arranging the other items, she removed her sandals and stood among them on the cloth. She draped the red ribbon across her palms and raised her hands. With great feeling, thinking about each phrase, she prayed, "Meciful Life-Lenders, I have done all you have required of me. I beg you to send my life-guide to keep me safe from the Death Stealers and their Sneaks. Let my guide come and make me complete."

Nothing happened.

She repeated the prayer, trying to put her whole soul into its expression. A seabird wheeled toward her. Her life-guide? She waited for a voice to speak in her mind and identify itself.

With a raucous cry the bird flew away over the water, proving itself just an ordinary gull that had hoped for a handout.

Perhaps it took time for the Life-Lenders to receive her plea and act on it and for the life-guide to make its way to her. Praying for patience, she waited.

It was a long and fruitless wait. The sun climbed to its highest point and began its slow descent. She cried out to the Life Lenders, begging them to hear her plea, lifting her hands high until her arms tired and fell to her sides.

Nothing answered her plea. No beast or bird or other creature that she alone could see took shape within the circle or outside it. She was alone with the beckoning cliff, the sea birds that wheeled high above it, and the relentless waves that beat on the rocks below.

# 2

# TRUTH

As the afternoon shadows deepened, Serollyn grew desperate, screaming to the Life Lenders to send her life-guide. Her cries went unanswered. In some way that she could not understand, she had failed the Life Lenders and been spurned.

With night approaching she stepped wearily from the circle, gathered up the cloth and its contents, and trudged back to the village. If her slumped shoulders and dragging feet didn't convey the message she could not bear to speak, her hair, still streaming loose and in wild disarray from the wind's buffeting, made her failure evident.

She felt more than saw the eyes that turned away in pity as she passed. Women grinding grain bent their backs to the task and pretended to be too busy to look up. Men skinning dassies caught in hunters' traps turned their backs and wielded their knives more fiercely. If any of her age-mates were about, they must have hidden themselves; not one of her friends came to offer comfort. Only the youngest children stared openly at the one denied by the Life Lenders.

She could not bear to return to the clan house. Instead she ran to the house she shared with Grandmother Sudy and dropped the sacred cloth and its contents onto the hard earth floor.

Sudy stood by her fireplace stirring pottage in an iron kettle hung over the fire. It would be her contribution to the clan's communal evening meal. The rich smell of simmering roots and herbs that rose from the mixture had no power to rouse Serollyn's appetite.

When Sudy turned toward her, the tears Serollyn had been holding back burst forth. She sank down on Sudy's sleeping furs and sobbed.

Sudy clucked sympathetically but did nothing to comfort her. When her grief had spent itself, Serollyn looked up to see that her grandmother had resumed her stirring.

"Grandmother," she said, "I did all the right things, I was ever so careful with the ritual, and no life-guide came. Why? Why didn't the Life Lenders send me my guide? Do they hate me? Will I be taken by the Death Stealers?"

Her grandmother sighed and took her stirrer from the pot. "Close the door, child," she said as she placed the long wooden paddle on a plate on her one table.

Serollyn got up and did as she was told, though with the door closed the fire's heat would soon make the small room unbearable.

When she returned to her seat, her grandmother said, "As to what will happen to you in the future, I cannot say. But we must talk of the present.

"Each of your age-mates returned to the village with a life-guide. They have boasted to you of the guides that answered their summons, have they not?"

Sudy knew well enough that it was so. But her grandmother regarded her closely, waiting for her answer.

"You know that they have," Serollyn said.

"Your close friends—Marleon, Nestryn, and Vali— they have life-guides?"

Serollyn shifted about uncomfortably, unable to imagine why her grandmother was putting her through this painful inquisition. "Of course they do," she said impatiently.

"Tell me what those guides look like," Sudy ordered.

Difficult as it was for her to speak of these things, she could not disregard Sudy's direct command. She had always obeyed her grandmother, always relied on her wisdom and, more importantly, on her love.

"Marleon's guide is a great-cat, tawny with white ear-tufts and a white tip on his tail. His eyes are green as sea-grass."

She picked up a large dried fern-frond and fanned herself for a moment before continuing. "Nestryn's guide is a brown monkey with a curly tail. Vali's ..." she paused, fighting back tears, composed herself, and continued, "Vali says hers is a small, dark man, his back hunched and his ears pointed like a deer's."

Her grandmother nodded as though approving these descriptions. "Life-guides have frequently appeared in all these forms, although, of course, each is distinctive in some way. Still, many of our people have had guides in the form of great-cats. Several have had those resembling some type of forest monkey. And although the little dark men are much less common, they are not unknown.

"Does anything mark these guides that you have described as being distinct from those of others? Have you noted unusual or distinctive characteristics in their appearance?"

Sweat trickled down Serollyn's face and arms, and she suspected that the heat might be affecting her grandmother's mind as well. "Grandmother Sudy," she said carefully, not wishing to offend the old woman, "why do you ask? You know that I can't see my friends' guides."

"Ah," said her grandmother, as though she had spoken some profound truth. "You have not seen these life-guides that you described."

"No, of course not. I was only repeating the descriptions that Marleon, Nestryn, and Vali gave me— gave us all."

"Just so." Her grandmother turned, took up the wooden paddle, and gave the mixture in the kettle a vigorous stirring, though how she could stand to be so close to the fire, Serollyn could not imagine.

After a moment or two, Sudy turned back to her. "Have you ever seen *anyone's* life-guide? A guide of one of the elders, perhaps?"

Serollyn shook her head. She was losing patience. "How could I, when a guide can be seen only by the one to whom it is sent."

"I know that you've been taught that life-guides show themselves only to the ones they choose," Sudy said. "What you have not been told is that a life-guide who so wishes, can under very special circumstances become visible to others."

"But Grandmother, that can't be. The elders would have taught us something so important. And I don't know of anybody who's ever seen someone else's life-guide. Have you? Really?"

Her grandmother smiled. "I'm going to show you something."

Again Sudy set the paddle on its rest. She picked up cloths, wrapped them around the handle of her kettle, and lifted it off the fire. Serollyn jumped up to help her, but her grandmother easily swung the heavy kettle around and set it onto the table.

"Look into the fire, my dear," her grandmother said, pointing at the dancing flames.

Serollyn's gaze followed the pointing finger and lighted on a large lizard curled on the burning logs. It blinked its golden eyes as though it winked at her. A long, forked tongue darted from its mouth. Serollyn screamed and looked away, blinking.

Her grandmother said, "That is Jec, my guide. Can you describe him now that you've seen him?"

Serollyn looked back at the fire but saw only the dying blaze. Dizzy and suddenly nauseated from the heat, she could scarcely breathe.

What *had* she seen? A lizard the color of fire? Or a mirage born of heat and vertigo? She could barely recall that brief vision. "It was some kind of lizard, big, I think." She was no longer sure of its size.

"Its eyes ..." Its eyes had scared her, but she could not now say why. They had reminded her—of what? Sparks cast off from the burning wood?

The tongue—what had it truly been like? Maybe like that small, blackened branch sticking out from a half-burned log in the hearth.

"I don't know, Grandmother. It wasn't clear." Thinking about it made her head swim again. "Did I really see it? How could I?"

"I allowed Jec to draw life from me for that moment that he was visible. Few of us still know how to do that."

Sudy pressed a cup against her lips. "Drink, child."

She took deep swallows of cool water, and gradually her head cleared. "I don't understand what seeing Jec has to do with me and with my guide not coming."

"Listen to me carefully," her grandmother said. "If someone knows that his or her place in the clan depends on successfully summoning a life-guide, and that someone also believes that no one else can see the life-guide, and that someone has heard many guides described and has only to recall one of those descriptions and alter it slightly, such a one might return from performing the summoning ritual and claim to have received a guide and give a convincing description, though no guide has appeared."

Serollyn stared stupidly at her grandmother. "Are you saying my friends lied? Their life-guides aren't real? They made up the descriptions?"

Her grandmother did not answer.

"It can't be true. *You* would have known. The other elders would have. They'd have punished anyone who lied."

"Serollyn, I could show you a quick glimpse of my life-guide. I haven't the power to see the life-guides of others."

"Then you don't know that anyone has lied about having a guide. So why are you saying that?"

"Because I suspect it's true. I can't bring charges; I have no proof, nor can I get any. But long ago, when I was young and Jec had only just come to me, a dear friend of mine came back from her ritual and described her life-guide to the clan, and everyone was happy for her. But the next day she came to me in private and said she had something to tell me, but first I must promise to keep her secret forever. Foolishly, having no idea what she was about to say, I promised. And she told me that no guide had come to her; she had lied to the clan, describing a life-guide that did not exist. She told me she'd gotten the idea from a friend, older than she, who confessed to her that he'd made up his life-guide.

"Horrified as I was, I kept my word. I have never revealed what she told me. But often through the years I wondered whether others besides my friend invented a guide they did not have. I noticed that sometimes a young person's description of a newly received guide would be too smooth, too detailed. But I kept silent.

"Eventually I married and had a son—your father. By the time he was of age to receive his life-guide, I suspected that many in the clan were claiming life-guides they did not have. Your father went through the ritual with the same result you have had—no life guide came to him. He swore he would take his life as Kreia later did. To save him I told him my suspicions, and to my great shame I urged him to do what my friend had done so many years before."

*No!* Serollyn's hands grasped the bed cover as though her grip could anchor her to reality. Against her will, not wanting to hear the answer, she asked, "And did he?"

Grandmother Sudy bowed her head. "He did."

"And now you want me to do the same?"

"No!" Sudy picked up the paddle with which she had stirred her kettle and brandished it near Serollyn's face. "No, you must not! Why do you think your father died in a hunting accident? Don't you know how rare such a death is? Your father's lie opened him to attack by the Death Stealers. They use tragic and painful means to snatch a life

14

that should have returned to the Life Lenders. You must never, never stoop to such deception. Your mother knew of his lie, and when she received the news of his death, shame and grief crazed her, driving her to flee from the clan.

Her father dead, her mother driven into exile—both destroyed by this monstrous lie. Serollyn's stomach churned. She staggered to her feet, rushed to the door, and threw it open. She got no more than a few steps before she fell to her knees and vomited the water she'd drunk. When her stomach finished heaving, she rose and, not looking around to see whether anyone had witnessed her shame, ran out of the village and into the woods beyond.

She ran until she stumbled and fell over a tree root. She lay still for a while, fighting for breath, and when enough strength returned, she crawled a short distance away, and collapsed onto a carpet of moss. There she huddled in misery, hearing again her grandmother's words.

Her father had lied about having a life-guide, and the lie had killed him! And driven her mother from the clan!

Some of her friends might also have lied.

No! Her friends would not lie about their guides. Never would Nestryn deceive her; she and Serollyn had been inseparable since they were toddlers. Marleon's sister was wed to Corlon, Serollyn's only brother, making Marleon her kin-by-marriage, as well as a life-long friend. He was like a brother to her, closer than she and Corlon had ever been.

And Vali, who'd sat at her side as they listened to the lessons of the elders. She recalled how Vali had tried to talk to her this morning and she had refused to listen.

Could Vali's tales of her life-guide be false? Is that what Vali had wanted to tell her?

Her grandmother should have told her these things before. Sudy had always taught her to be truthful, yet she had not been truthful with Serollyn. How could Sudy have participated in such a huge and terrible deception?

Especially when she was not part of it. Sudy really had a life-guide. She'd seen him. But how was it possible to see someone else's life-guide?

*Had* she truly seen something in her grandmother's fire?

## 3

# LIFE-GUIDE

Serollyn must have fainted or perhaps only fallen asleep. It was night when she awoke, roused by the snuffling of a large animal. She sat up and peered into the darkness. Krissa, the larger moon, had not yet risen, and Benat, the smaller moon, gave only enough light to show the vague outlines of shrubs and trees, too little to provide a clue to her location or the direction she should take to get back to the village.

And the sound was coming nearer.

This wood was not like the vast forests that lay farther to the east, away from the sea. It held no great-cats or orsas. The only dangerous creatures in the wood were wild boars, but those were fierce enough, and she had no desire to encounter one, alone and unarmed.

She rose quietly to her feet. The snuffling stopped with a suspicious suddenness. She moved slowly toward a large tree. A dark shape charged out of the bushes and rushed toward her.

She leaped for the tree and jumped behind it. The animal dashed past. It was the largest boar she'd ever seen. Moonlight gleamed on its fearsome tusks. It had to be a Sneak sent by the Death Stealers! Because she'd failed to receive a life-guide, the Death Stealers were claiming her.

The boar skidded to a halt, wheeled, and headed back toward her. This time it stopped before reaching the tree. It pawed the ground and stared at her, its beady eyes glowing even in the dim moonlight.

That greedy gaze caught and held her. The boar blurred into motion. A red haze enveloped her. Her back thudded against the hard ground. Pain lanced her body.

Sorrow, loss, regret blasted into her with the boar's steamy breath. Her own breath came in desperate and diminishing gasps. Then in a death dream, a yellow streak hurtled toward the boar.

The yellow form, barely discernible through her haze of blood and pain, launched itself onto the boar's back. The boar whirled, tried to jab its tusks into its attacker.

A dog, Serollyn saw. Her would-be rescuer was a dog. It sank its teeth into the boar's shoulder and clung to its back, out of reach of the tusks. Trying to shake the dog off, the boar ran for the bushes. The dog slipped off when the boar tunneled beneath low hanging branches. She saw it clearly now. Panting, it watched the retreating boar.

As Serollyn stared, the dog turned toward her, tongue lolling, tail wagging. It trotted to her and sank onto its haunches, its golden eyes staring into hers.

She sat up, a bit surprised that she could. She'd been so sure ...

There were scratches on her arms, and blood on her wraparound almost concealed the large tear at her waist. Yet her probing fingers found no wound beneath the torn cloth.

She'd thought …

She'd felt …

But no tusk could have penetrated her body. The Sneak, if that was what the boar had been, had failed.

She stretched her hand toward the dog, and it leaned forward and licked her palm. *It seems I got here just in time,* a voice spoke in her mind. *I'm Krannel. I'm sent to be your life-guide.*

"My *life-guide!* Oh, thanks be to the Life Lenders! And thank *you,* Krannel, for saving me from that boar! You … you did more than just chase it away. I mean … I was gored. I thought … Iwas sure I was dying. But I'm not hurt. Did you …?"

*The Life Lenders made it possible for me to share my life with you. I can say no more.*

"But why didn't you come when I performed the ritual? Was it some kind of test?"

*In a way. Let's just say I was delayed.*

"But why? How?"

*Does it matter? I came when you most needed me.*

"And I'm so glad. But I have so many questions."

*I am not here to answer your questions but to help you find your own answers.*

Afraid Krannel would vanish if she closed her eyes, she talked, at first of inconsequential things, of her relief at being alive, and then, with growing confidence, of her hopes and fears, her dreams and disappointments, even whispering her vague hope of finding her mother, and finally she spoke of the terrible revelation that had driven her into the woods. She talked until she fell asleep, and when she awakened and saw Krannel lying near her, she felt complete. Her life-guide had come. He was real, not a dream born of her brush with death.

Proudly she braided her long hair into a single braid. Lacking the red ribbon, she broke off a length of supple vine and tied it around the braid's end to secure it. She adjusted her wraparound so that the tear with its ugly bloodstain was on one side and less noticeable.

In her morning prayers she poured out thanks to the Life Lenders for sparing her life and for sending Krannel to be her life-guide. She finished her prayers well past sunrise and rose a bit stiffly from the damp ground to return to the village in triumph, to proclaim the arrival of her life-guide.

As she walked proudly into the village, Krannel frolicked at her side. She could see him so clearly in the bright light of day—a large dog, nondescript yellow with smudges of dark brown along both sides and more clearly defined brown on the tips of his ears and tail—that it was hard to believe that he would be invisible to all but her.

She wanted Sudy to be the first to know about Krannel. But Sudy would not be home. She would be at the great house where the clan would be gathered for their communal breakfast. As they approached the great house, she pointed out to Krannel how the early morning sunlight gilded the high peaked roof, a familiar sight that acquired fresh beauty now that she could share it with her guide. From within the long wooden building came the clatter of utensils, the buzz of conversations, the merry whistle of a reed flute—happy sounds she'd known all her life but loved the more with Krannel at her side.

Her mouth watered at the aroma of fresh baked bread and fried fish cakes that wafted toward her through the open windows. She couldn't remember when she'd had such an appetite. She'd eaten nothing the day before and could hardly wait until she'd shared her glad news with the clan and could set to on the food.

She bounced into the room smiling broadly and waved a greeting to her age-mates, gathered in the common hall breaking fast with their elders after completing the early morning family chores and before heading out on their clan-assigned tasks. Nestryn and Vali sat together, her own place empty beside them. She headed toward them.

"Here, what do you mean, bringing that ugly cur into the eating room?" The harsh voice of the clan mother wiped the smile from Serollyn's face.

"You ... you can see him?" she stammered in shocked surprise. "He's Krannel, my life-guide. He came to me last night."

Silence fell over the group, broken when someone giggled. Others joined the laughter, while an elder stood and called out, "You really think you can pass that sorry mongrel off as a life-guide? Why, we can all see him."

"But ... but he *is*. He saved me from a boar. He—"

Catcalls and jeers drowned her words.

She looked around, seeking support among her friends. Nestryn and Vali avoided her gaze, but she was amazed to see a small, brown monkey perched on Nestryn's shoulder. Her life-guide! Her friend hadn't lied.

She pointed at the monkey. "I see your life-guide, Nestryn," she called out. "Why shouldn't you see mine?"

"No one sees any life-guide but his own," another of the elders spoke up. "How could you think we would be taken in by such a blasphemous ruse?"

She scarcely heard him, too busy surveying the room

to observe what had never before been visible to her.

Often she had heard the clan members describe their life-guides. Now she saw on shoulders, on laps, standing next to their companions, sitting on the table beside their breakfast bowl, the beings that matched those descriptions.

Along with Nestryn's monkey, she saw her brother Corlon's shaggy-coated orsa, Corlon's wife Laki's gentle dove, the chief elder's golden hawk, another elder's long-nosed moon rat, the piper's graceful gazelle. And Sudy's fire lizard. Her grandmother stood and was making her way toward her from across the room, Jec on her shoulder, his tail curled gracefully around her neck.

What struck her with a force that drove away her hunger was the number of guides she did not see. Where was the seabird that Nestryn's sister Katyn described in loving detail down to the last feather? Where was the vervex with back-curved horns that Katyn's husband Ubon boasted so about? Why did she see no great-cat crouched beside Marleon? Where was Vali's small dark man?

Even some of the elders seemed to be without guides. She did not see old Morkle's basilisk. And hard as she tried, she could not find the clan mother's golden phoenix.

*I can see life-guides, Krannel,* she mindspoke. *But only some of them.*

*You see all that are here,* came the answer she had dreaded.

That horrifying revelation made her oblivious to the cries of "Shame!" and "She's a disgrace to the clan," until she heard Marleon's voice raised along with the others. "Shame!" he was shouting, "She's shaming us all."

22

Someone grabbed the end of her braid and yanked off the tie she'd improvised. The braid unraveled and her hair again hung free like a child's.

*The real life-guides will let their people know that I'm telling the truth, won't they?* she sent urgently. *And then they'll know the truth about the others.*

*The life-guides will keep silence,* Krannel returned. *It is up to you to convince the clan.*

Serollyn could not believe the injustice of that decree. She would have objected, but her grandmother reached her side. "You'd best go home," Sudy said. "They're in no mood to listen to reason. I'll come to you as soon as I can. Hurry, while I try to calm things down."

Serollyn left, urged on by Krannel, who barked and snapped to clear a way for her through the crowded room. Once outside, Serollyn dashed home, spurred on less by the taunts and threats of the clan than by the horror of the lies her unexpected and unprecedented gift revealed.

Only when she reached the cottage and slammed the door shut behind her did she give way to the tears that had been building up during her flight. They were tears of anger more than grief, and she let some of that anger spill onto Krannel.

"Why didn't you help me back there?" she demanded. "You could've done something to prove what you are. And *why* won't the other life-guides tell their people the truth?"

Krannel sat on his haunches and looked up at her, ears erect. He said nothing.

"So now you're playing the dumb dog they accused you of being." The heat of her anger dried her tears. "Why are you doing this to me?"

His answer was a low growl.

"Oh, I'm not supposed to question you, is that it?"

He bared his teeth in what looked suspiciously like a grin but still did not speak.

"How can I ever make anyone believe me if you're going to act like this?"

His tail thumped once against the floor.

"All right, ignore me then." Serollyn turned her back to him, positioning herself to face the open door and watch for her grandmother.

She didn't have long to wait. Krannel had still not broken his silence when Sudy entered the house and pulled the door shut behind her. She walked toward the fireplace, and Jec leaped from her shoulder into the cold ashes.

"Well, that certainly stirred things up," she announced in a tone more satisfied than consoling.

"But what's happening?" Serollyn cried. "Why could they all see Krannel? And how could I see their life-guides—the ones that had them?" This last she added bitterly, still trying to grasp the enormity of the deception practiced by so many.

"What does Krannel say about that?" Sudy asked, eyeing the dog.

"Nothing! He won't even talk to me." Serollyn's tears began to flow again. "Maybe I just dreamed that he was a life-guide. Maybe they're right, and he is just an old yellow mongrel."

Krannel snarled and snapped in Serollyn's direction, though he wasn't close enough to touch her.

"That's a silly thing to say," Sudy said mildly. "Especially after the gift the Life Lenders gave you."

"Gift?"

"Of seeing all the life-guides. Don't you know what a

privilege you were granted?"

"Privilege? Everybody thinks I'm a liar and a cheat. Even the ones with guides. Krannel says their life-guides won't tell them any different. What use is it to have a guide who didn't help when everybody was accusing me and laughing at me?"

Krannel cast her a disdainful look, rose, and walked to the door. He stood looking out and wagging his tail.

"Serollyn!" Sudy shook a finger in her face. "Never, never insult your life-guide."

*It's all right. She's had a severe shock. She'll need time to recover.* Serollyn heard Krannel's words clearly in her mind, yet they were directed to Sudy, and Sudy's nod told Serollyn she'd heard them. So his speech as well as his appearance was not to be exclusively hers.

"Why are you so different from the other guides?" she demanded. "Are the Life Lenders playing some kind of joke on me?"

"The Life Lenders don't play jokes," Sudy said sharply. "You've always revered them. Trust them now."

Krannel's tail wagged faster. *Someone's coming,* he announced.

# 4

# BELIEVER

"Close the door, Grandmother," Serollyn begged. "I don't want to see anybody. Not now."

But Krannel was blocking the doorway and made no attempt to move. Sudy looked out past him. "Too late," she said. "It's Vali. She's almost here."

She'd scarcely said the words when Vali bounced into Serollyn's line of sight. Serollyn groaned. Close friends though they were, she knew what a gossip Vali was and guessed that Vali had come to gather fresh news to spread.

On the other hand, Vali's coming could be a good thing. If Krannel would reveal his identity to her, Vali would waste no time spreading the word. So Serollyn wiped the tears from her eyes and cheeks and mustered a smile as Vali poked her head into the room.

Vali looked askance at Krannel, who had not moved and was blocking her path. "He won't bite, will he?"

"Of course not," Serollyn replied. "He's wagging his tail, so he must be pleased to see you."

Vali stepped carefully around and past him to enter the small room. Sudy moved back against the fireplace, out of the way.

"That was quite a performance," Vali said. "I can't

believe you thought you'd get away with it. You know, I tried to warn you yesterday morning, but you wouldn't listen. You should have—I'd've helped you come up with a convincing story." She broke into a laugh. "I have to say, though, that was a stunt nobody else'd ever think of."

"It wasn't a stunt," Serollyn began angrily.

A low growl from Krannel warned her to stop, control her anger, and start again. After taking a deep breath, she said, "Vali, I guess it does look to you and Marleon like I was pulling some kind of joke. But don't you know me well enough to know I wouldn't do that?"

"Oh, come on, Serollyn," Vali said. "We can all see that dog. He can't be a life-guide."

"He is, though," Serollyn insisted. "I don't understand it, either."

"Well, there, that proves it!" Vali gave her a triumphant look. "A real guide would explain things, wouldn't it?"

Serollyn lost patience. "How would you know?" she asked. "You don't have one."

"Prove it," Vali said, her eyes narrowing, her smile gone.

"I can't see him," Serollyn responded. "I can see all the life-guides, and your Veral just isn't there. Neither is Marleon's great-cat. Neither are a lot of the others."

"Nobody can see other people's guides."

"I can. I don't know how or why, but I can. I can see Grandmother Sudy's fire lizard, and I saw Nestryn's monkey and the chief elder's golden hawk and—"

"You're making it all up," Vali declared. "It isn't funny anymore. I'm going."

She spun around and flounced from the hut. When

Serollyn would have called after her, Sudy put a hand on her arm. "Let her go," she advised.

Serollyn watched Vali's haughty retreat, and her tears welled up again. "What will I do if I can't make anyone believe me?"

She'd addressed the question to Sudy, but Krannel answered. *You have to convince them. Tears won't help.*

It took two days for Serollyn to gather the courage to act on Krannel's advice, two days of keeping herself hidden in the cottage, eating her meals there, refusing to join the communal morning and evening meals. Krannel stayed with her and shared the food Sudy prepared, but her grandmother went off each day to take her place in the community. As a member of the council, Sudy had responsibilities to the entire clan, not just to her granddaughter.

If Krannel had offered more in the way of advice and encouragement, Serollyn told herself that she could have endured the scorn of the clan more easily. But he said little, merely told her she had to work through things herself, and he would wait patiently while she did so.

So she fumed and wept and prayed to the Life Lenders for guidance, and, finally, resolved to try to convince one other person that she was telling the truth. She decided to talk to Nestryn.

To do so she had to leave the refuge of Sudy's cottage. The prospect frightened her, but she gathered her courage, and waited for an opportunity to find Nestryn alone. She and Nestryn had always been close friends; she knew Nestryn's habits as well as her own.

Skilled at basketwork, Nestryn would go on certain

days to the marsh to gather the tough fronds of marsh grass, which she would dry and weave into baskets. Serollyn sometimes accompanied her friend on these expeditions. Nestryn knew the waterways and hummocks well and could find her way through shallow water and from dry ground to dry ground. She always said she loved the noisy peacefulness: the cries of marsh birds and the whir of wings when a startled bird took flight, the constant hum of insects, the plop of a frog jumping off a log into the water, the constant drip-drip of water falling from moisture-laden leaves.

Serollyn enjoyed these things, too, but not with the same passion that imbued Nestryn. She took them for granted and took special note of them only when Nestryn rhapsodized over them. They held no appeal for her now. She only knew that in the marsh she could talk to Nestryn without fear of being overheard or interrupted. With Krannel to help her, Serollyn was confident of finding her friend easily.

She pulled her high sharkskin boots on over bare feet and slipped on a poncho woven of the large water-shedding leaves of the scrub palm. A conical hat of the same leaves not only offered additional protection but also served to hide her face as she passed through the village. With Krannel frolicking beside her, she could hardly go unnoticed or unrecognized. However, she could avoid meeting anyone's gaze, and she ignored the occasional catcalls.

Once they reached the marsh, Krannel took the lead and with only a little sniffing around picked up and followed Nestryn's trail. They found Nestryn seated on a wide tree root, her basket of marsh grass beside her.

Engrossed in watching a female water spider wind strands of pearly eggs around a tall reed, she seemed not to hear them coming.

Tolammy had heard them. Perched on a low-hanging branch of the same tree whose root served Nestryn as a seat, the small brown monkey turned as they neared and regarded them with a quizzical expression.

"Hello, Nestryn. Hello, Tolammy," Serollyn called out.

Nestryn jumped from the root with a loud splash and whirled around to face them.

"Sorry if I startled you," Serollyn said. "I came out here to talk to you."

"About your supposed life-guide?" Nestryn's lip curled.

"About Krannel, yes. And other things."

"Serollyn, we've been friends all our lives," Nestryn said, climbing over the root and sitting down on it again, facing Serollyn. "I thought I knew you almost as well as I know myself, but I can't understand why you'd tell such a wild story. Did Vali put you up to it?"

"Nobody put me up to it. You know me so well—you should know I'm telling the truth. Krannel *is* my life-guide. I don't understand why everyone can see him. Or why I can see everyone's guide now."

"That can't be true," Nestryn said, frowning. "If it were, you would understand because your guide would explain it. And if it were true, our guides would have told us. Tolammy hasn't said anything to me, and I'm sure no one else's guides have said anything, either."

"That's another thing I don't understand. Krannel doesn't explain much. Not that I don't ask him, but he just tells me I have to figure things out for myself."

Nestryn snorted. "How convenient," she said. "And

what have you figured out so far?"

"That you don't believe me," Serollyn said. "And," she added, "how to make you believe me."

"How?"

"I can describe what Tolammy is doing right now. He's on the branch over your head making faces at Krannel."

Nestryn looked up. "Good guess," she said. "He's on the branch, but he's not making faces."

"He was, before you looked at him. Now he's jumping off the branch onto your shoulder. He's wrapped his tail around your neck, and he just stuck out his tongue at me."

Nestryn's surprised look told Serollyn she was making progress.

"Those couldn't have been lucky guesses," Serollyn said. "Tolammy just told you to keep an open mind."

Nestryn's jaw dropped. "You can *hear* him, too?"

"I didn't know I could, but I did."

"But this is all so impossible," Nestryn said, kicking her feet in the water.

"I know, but it *is* true," Serollyn said, moving back to keep from being splashed.

"Have Krannel speak to me," Nestryn said. "Then I'll believe it all."

"I can't get Krannel to do anything he doesn't want to do. He just says he's my guide, I'm not his."

A puzzled frown creased Nestryn's forehead. "But doesn't he want people to believe you?"

"I'm not sure what he wants," Serollyn said with a sigh. "He speaks in riddles a lot. And sometimes he doesn't speak at all."

Krannel wagged his tail, perhaps in assent, perhaps

just in doggy playfulness. He went bounding after a water snake winding its way through the marsh grass.

Watching him, Nestryn said, "I'm sorry, Serollyn, but it's hard to believe he's anything more than a dog."

"If people could see Tolammy and judge by the way he acts, would they think he was anything more than a monkey?"

"Of course they would," Nestryn exclaimed, indignant.

Tolammy caught hold of her braid and swung on it. She yelled and grabbed for him.

"Of course they would," Serollyn mimicked, laughing.

Tolammy dodged Nestryn's grasp and yanked out the ribbon wound through her braid, freeing her hair. "Stop that!" she said. "Now I've got to braid it all over again." To Serollyn she said, "He never acts like that."

"So maybe he wants to prove my point," Serollyn said.

Tolammy released Nestryn's hair but kept the ribbon and leaped up into the tree with it, chittering as he wrapped the ribbon around his body.

Serollyn described his actions to Nestryn, whose flushed cheeks revealed her embarrassment.

"Of course you can see the ribbon, but I guess you really can see him," Nestryn admitted. "He must want you to. He only plays like this when we're alone. With others in the clan he does nothing that would confirm his presence, just rides on my shoulder and behaves as a life-guide should."

"Which Krannel just won't do," Serollyn said. "Everybody sees him, and they see him acting like a dog. I guess it's natural that they don't believe me."

With a big splash Krannel pounced at the spot where the snake had been, but it disappeared beneath the water and surfaced a good distance away. With a disgusted snort, Krannel turned back toward Serollyn and Nestryn.

"Krannel, please speak to Nestryn," Serollyn begged.

*It isn't necessary. She's ready to believe you now.*

Cocking his head, he looked up at Tolammy, and Serollyn was certain that a communication passed between them, though she was not privy to it and neither, she suspected, was Nestryn.

Tolammy jumped onto Nestryn's shoulder but paused only long enough to put into her hand the red ribbon he'd stolen. He leaped from her shoulder onto Krannel's back.

*Follow us,* came Krannel's instruction to Serollyn. She heard Tolammy give the same instruction to Nestryn, but so far as she could tell, Nestryn hadn't heard Krannel.

Nestryn looked inquiringly at Serollyn. "They say we're to follow them," Serollyn said. "We'd better do it."

Nestryn gathered up her basket of marsh grass, and she and Serollyn trailed along after their guides.

# 5

# RESCUE

"Any idea where we're going?" Serollyn asked when they veered away from the village.

"I'd guess we're looking for Marleon," Nestryn answered, glancing upward at the cloudy sky. "We're going toward the beach, and the fishing boats will be coming in at any time. He went out alone in that little boat he's so proud of, and there's a storm brewing."

Serollyn hadn't noticed the change in the weather. In the marsh the trees hid the gathering clouds. Afternoon storms were frequent at this time of year, and the fishing crews kept close watch for them and headed for the beach when the clouds gathered and the wind picked up. Although her anger at Marleon for not believing her and for having lied about having a life-guide had not lessened, she did not want to see him in grave danger, as he well could be, with no life-guide to protect him.

As they neared the beach, they passed men and a few women hurrying toward the village. "Bad storm's coming up," one man called out to them. "Best turn back. All the crews are coming in."

They did not turn back, and the man who'd given the warning didn't linger to see if they followed his advice.

34

Serollyn scanned each passing face, looking for Marleon. "Why isn't he in yet?" she wondered aloud.

"He's a strong rower," Nestryn answered. "Sometimes he goes out farther than he should, takes chances he shouldn't. The fool thinks if he impresses the other men with his courage, they'll let him go with a hunting party."

The rain started, a light drizzle that quickly coalesced into large, pounding drops that fell faster and faster until it seemed that a waterfall was pouring down on them. A wind came up, tore off Serollyn's woven hat, and carried it away. No time to go after it. She and Nestryn raced along. She could no longer see Krannel in front of them. With rain pouring against her it was hard to breathe, and she fought the wind that tried to push her back, away from her goal.

Jagged bursts of lightning illuminated the beach just ahead of them. They threaded their way through inverted canoes tethered to palms growing well above the high tide mark and whipping about in frenzied dance. Without question, in this storm, tossed about in his small boat, Marleon courted death. Could the Death Stealers have brought this storm as punishment for him? She breathed a frantic prayer to the Life Lenders as they made their way closer to the shoreline.

Something fell from a palm as they passed it, startling a scream from Serollyn. But it was only Tolammy, jumping onto Nestryn's shoulder and throwing his arms around her neck to cling to her as she ran.

"Where's Krannel?" Serollyn managed between gasps for breath.

*In the water*, came Tolammy's disquieting reply. *He's trying to save your foolhardy friend.*

"He says—" Nestryn began.

"I heard." Serollyn dashed to the water's edge.

Waves broke around and over her, their crashes competing with the booming thunder. The roiling black clouds made it difficult to see, except in the lightning flashes

Ignoring the rushing water that threatened to sweep her off her feet, Serollyn strained to catch sight through the gloom of a glimpse of yellow fur. Her concern now was all for Krannel, her erstwhile anguish over Marleon forgotten. She absolutely could not lose her life-guide.

Nestryn caught up to her but stood behind her. Serollyn's brief glance revealed Tolammy perched on Nestryn's shoulder, a shivering mass of soaked monkey. Serollyn heard Nestryn shout some warning, but the words were lost in the storm's tumult.

Her own words would be just as lost to Nestryn, but Tolammy could hear her thought. "Do you know where Krannel is? Is he safe? He can't be killed—can he?"

*Safe? Hardly. And yes, Krannel can be killed. Any of us can under certain circumstances, but Krannel is especially vulnerable. But he's alive. He's strong; he's fighting the current. Have faith.*

Again Serollyn breathed a silent prayer to the Life Lenders, this time for Krannel: *Bring him back to me. Don't let me lose my life-guide just after getting him.*

"Krannel, can you hear me?" she shouted into the wind.

No answer came. With a roar like a great-cat, the wind tore at her. A wave hit her with a force that shoved her back against Nestryn, toppling them both. The receding water dragged them with it into the churning surf.

Serollyn got herself turned, dug her fingers into the

sand, and clawed her way back, her knees scraping on shells. She looked around for Nestryn, saw Tolammy tug her by the hair, dragging her to safety.

Sneezing and spitting salt water, Serollyn flopped beside her but rested only a moment before struggling to her feet and peering again at the raging waters. Nestryn's basket of marsh grasses rocked on the crest of a wave, toppled, and was swept out to sea.

In the distance a lightening of the sky indicated that the storm might be easing. As Serollyn continued to pray, the thunder faded into the distance and the noise of the storm lessened.

With a plop the waves spat out some unwanted prey and retreated, leaving the soggy mass behind. Yellow fur and brown flesh caught her eye. She ran to it, Nestryn following.

She, Nestryn, and Tolammy disentangled dog and person and pulled both out of reach of the hungry waves.

Krannel whined. He was alive! Serollyn threw herself on him, embracing him, tears mixing with the rain.

*Look to Marleon,* came her life-guide's mental order.

Nestryn was already bending over their friend, pounding on his chest. Tolammy patted Nestryn's arm, and Serollyn felt the calm he urged on them both.

"He's not breathing," Nestryn cried.

Tolammy told her to press down on Marleon's chest, hold, release, and press again.

To Serollyn he instructed, *Place your mouth over his and breathe into his lungs.*

Noting the blue tinge of Marleon's lips and cheeks, Serollyn feared the Death Stealers had already taken their vengeance. Nevertheless, she followed Tolammy's instructions. He had Serollyn hold Marleon's nose shut, press her mouth against his and breathe, release, and breathe again.

Marleon's sputtering cough and intake of breath rewarded their efforts. Color seeped back into his cheeks. He blinked, spat out seawater, and tried to sit up. Once again Krannel had cheated the Death Stealers of their prey.

Nestryn supported Marleon's back. He was shivering, so Serollyn stripped off her poncho and put it over him.

The storm had eased off while they were preoccupied with Marleon; the rain slowed to a steady, light shower.

"We need to get him home where he can get dry and warm," Nestryn said.

Serollyn agreed, but she had to see first to Krannel. He, like Marleon, was wet and shivering, and he gazed at her with bleary eyes. *It was a close thing for both of us,* he spoke in her mind. *I have to rest a bit. Go on, get your friend home. I'll follow when I can.*

"But you need to get out of the rain as much as he does," Serollyn objected, unwilling to leave her life-guide.

*The rain will stop soon.*

*I'll stay with him,* Tolammy said. *He'll be safe. You both go on and take Marleon home.*

"I've never been apart from you," Nestryn objected.

Tolammy waved his paw. *Many things are happening that have not happened before. Go on, I say. Krannel and I will be back with you shortly.*

Despite her obvious reluctance, Nestryn helped Serollyn get Marleon to his feet. Supported between them, his arms over their shoulders, he was able to move his feet enough to walk with them in a slow advance to the village.

As Serollyn walked home after completing her assigned tasks for the day she looked about, hoping to see Nestryn. She very much wanted to talk to her friend but had not seen her in the six days that had passed since they'd delivered Marleon into the care of his relieved family.

Probably Nestryn had not yet returned from gathering berries and nuts. Serollyn had finished her tasks early. They weren't onerous ones, only humiliating. Because the clan refused to believe that she had a life-guide, Serollyn was not considered an adult and was assigned tasks that were given to children. She swept the great house after the communal meals, fed and groomed the goats, and gathered palm fronds for thatching roofs. She had not needed to do that last task this day, and had finished the others early.

She considered stopping by Marleon's home, but he had recovered from his ordeal and was not likely to be there. Even if he was, she did not feel comfortable going there. He had not supported their story of how Krannel had saved his life. In truth, he couldn't: he'd been unconscious and had only awakened on the beach in the rain being ministered to by Nestryn and Serollyn, and that was what he'd told his family and the clan. No one believed Nestryn's claim that Krannel had saved him anymore than they believed that Krannel was a guide. It was likely, everyone said, that Marleon's great-cat had saved him.

So Serollyn found herself still shunned by the clan, and now Nestryn, too, was regarded with suspicion. Serollyn wanted to tell Nestryn how sorry she was about that, but the clan seemed bent on keeping her isolated from her friends as well as from younger children on whom she might exert an unwholesome influence. The future that had seemed so bright had turned hopeless and dark.

*You must be patient,* Krannel counseled, trotting along beside her as she returned to Sudy's cabin discouraged and disheartened. *Something will happen soon.*

"Something good?" Serollyn asked, eager for relief.

*Something. Whether good or bad you must decide.*

That was the sort of enigmatic comment that drove her mad. Having a life-guide was not what she'd expected. Instead of answers to her questions she got riddles; instead of advice he gave her choices and told her to decide which course was the wiser.

By the time she reached home she no longer felt like seeing or talking to anyone. She slammed into the house. Relieved that Sudy was not there, Serollyn crossed to the bed, prepared to throw herself onto it and have a good cry.

Startled by a light cough, she spun around. Marleon emerged from the shadows, looking shamefaced. "I didn't mean to scare you," he said. "I have to talk to you."

"What about?" The question came out more sharply than she'd intended. She didn't mean to be unkind to Marleon, but she was still angry with him.

He hung his head. "I should have come to thank you," he mumbled. "I would have, but ... well, that story, uh, about your dog saving me ... I didn't know what to think."

"Not my dog—my life-guide," she snapped.

Krannel settled down onto the floor between them and commenced scratching. Marleon frowned then grinned. "Sure looks like a dog to me," he said.

Krannel curled around and proceeded to lick and bite his flank. Serollyn was sure her life-guide was acting doglike on purpose.

"And isn't it too bad that I can't see what your great-cat is doing?" she said. "For all I know he's sharpening his claws on Grandmother Sudy's best chair. But then, you can't see what he's doing either, can you? Since he isn't here."

Marleon's face darkened. He headed for the door. "I shouldn't have come," he muttered.

"Wait." Serollyn hurried after him. "I'm sorry. I shouldn't have been rude. Not when you came to thank me."

He slowed, stopped, and turned to face her. "That isn't why I came," he said. "I mean, I know you helped me even though I don't know what happened after my boat overturned—what really happened."

Serollyn lost patience again. "Krannel swam out and pulled you in. You were drowning."

He looked at Krannel, who had followed Serollyn to the door. Krannel wagged his tail.

"Well, maybe," Marleon said.

"You certainly know that your great-cat didn't save you as some people are saying."

He nodded slowly. "I know," he said, not meeting her gaze.

"All right, never mind all that. Why did you come?"

Nervously he peered outside, then closed the door. "To warn you."

"Warn me? About what?" Serollyn stepped back, nearly tripping over Krannel. "You're being awfully mysterious," she said, sitting on the cot and motioning for him to take the chair.

He remained standing. "If I'm seen here, I'll be in trouble too."

41

"What kind of trouble?"

"Serollyn, some of the clan think you aren't being punished enough. They want to … they're planning to … to kill you."

"Kill me?" She jumped to her feet. "They want to *kill* me? Just because they don't believe me?"

His gaze fixed on his feet, Marleon kicked at the hard earth floor. "It's not that they don't believe you. They're afraid. The ones that want to kill you think you *are* telling the truth. That you can see who has life-guides and who doesn't. They're afraid you'll expose them."

"And how do you know this?" Serollyn demanded. "Why would they tell you?"

"Not 'they.' Just one," Marleon said, not lifting his gaze. "I can't tell you who."

"You don't have to. I can guess. Your grandfather, Old Morkle. He doesn't have a guide. I saw that."

He raised his head then and looked her in the eyes. "Serollyn, please, you've got to promise me you won't tell anyone. You mustn't expose him."

"Who'd believe me if I did tell?"

"The people that want to kill you. The ones with real life-guides, they wouldn't know you were telling the truth, but the ones who've lied, well, if you name them, they'll know you're right. And you have named some of them."

"Who? I could, but I haven't."

"You've named Vali. And me. And you've told Nestryn some of the others. So she's in danger, too."

"But they wouldn't really kill me—or Nestryn. I can't believe that."

"Look, maybe they wouldn't, but they are talking about it. I don't think you should take the chance."

She saw genuine anguish in his eyes. Marleon clearly believed that the threat was serious. "What should I do?" she asked.

Again he dropped his gaze and stared at the floor. "I don't know," he mumbled. "If that dog *is* your guide, ask him what to do."

"Marleon, look at me," she said. When he looked up, she continued, "Do *you* believe that Krannel is my life-guide?"

"I want to believe you," he said sheepishly as he looked away again.

"Do you? I know you made up your great-cat. You lied about something as important as that, so how can I believe you now? About anything?"

"I'm not lying about the danger. You have to believe that." He hesitated, then went on, "I'm sorry I lied to you about having a life-guide. Vali knew, and I think Nestryn did, but you—you've always been so devoted to the Life Lenders. I didn't know what you'd do if I told you. I didn't want you to hate me, and I didn't want you to run to tell the elders."

She wanted to protest that she would not have done that, but she wasn't sure what she might have done. So she said, "Marleon, I need you to believe me about Krannel. He did save your life. You must know that. I couldn't have, and Nestryn couldn't have, and your great-cat isn't real, so who else could have swum out into the storm and brought you to shore?"

Marleon looked at Krannel, who perked up his ears and wagged his tail.

"I guess that's right," he admitted. He bent and scratched the dog's head. "I guess I do owe you my life.

Thank you. I'm sorry I doubted you."

*Finally. That's what I wanted to hear.*

Marleon jumped. His eyes wide, he said, "I heard him. He spoke to me."

"You heard him?" Serollyn was as surprised as Marleon. "Even without a guide of your own?"

Still staring at Krannel, Marleon nodded. "What does it mean?" he whispered.

*It means you are chosen to help change things,* came the answer that Serollyn heard clearly, though it was directed to Marleon.

"How?" Marleon asked. "What am I supposed to do?"

*You've already done one thing. By warning Serollyn you've taken the first step. I think you know that by telling her you've put yourself in danger, too.*

"Oh, Marleon! I didn't think—"

"Don't worry about me," Marleon interrupted Serollyn's distressed cry. "Krannel's right. I knew what I was doing."

"So you, Nestryn, and I—we're all at risk."

"And him, too." Marleon nodded toward Krannel.

"He'll protect me. And Tolammy will protect Nestryn. But you—you have no protection."

Marleon regarded Krannel thoughtfully. "Can you? You and Tolammy? Can you protect them?"

*We can protect them against some dangers but not all. You've warned Serollyn about danger from the clan, but there are other dangers neither of you is aware of. If you help us, the protection against those will be stronger.*

"What are those dangers?" Serollyn asked.

*It is better that you do not know at this time. The knowledge would not protect you.*

"So what should we do?" Marleon sounded scared.

*That must be your decision.*

"Then I think … I think," he started slowly, hesitated, and then blurted, "I think we should hide somewhere."

"Hide?" Serollyn said. "Where? How?"

"I think," Marleon said, sounding more confident, "that we should go into the forest."

"Don't be silly! That's the most dangerous thing we could do."

*On the contrary, I think it's a wise solution,* Krannel said.

Marleon looked proud. As though it was all settled, he said, "I'll go get Nestryn."

# 6

# FOREST

Marleon led the way into the forest, following a path the hunters used. Krannel walked by his side, arousing a twinge of jealousy in Serollyn. She'd thought he was her life-guide, but it seemed he was anyone's. Tolammy didn't act that way. Although he sometimes spoke in her mind as well as in Nestryn's, he stayed with Nestryn, riding her shoulder. Whether Tolammy approved of this trek Serollyn couldn't tell. At least he hadn't opposed Nestryn's going.

It hadn't been as hard as Serollyn had expected to convince Nestryn that they should flee. Nestryn had always been curious about the forest and the unknown world beyond it, so she looked forward to the adventure. It was Serollyn who held back, unwilling either to leave her grandmother or to expose her friends to the forest's dangers.

When they all gathered in her small home and discussed Marleon's warning, Sudy said, "The danger is real. I could feel the tension in the great room this morning. Small groups were whispering together—the ones I suspect don't have life-guides. I don't know that they're planning to kill anyone, but they are planning something. I agree that it would be best for you to go away from here."

"But the forest is as dangerous as staying here," Serollyn objected.

"Not when you have your life-guide to protect you."

"Can't Krannel protect me just as well here as he could in the forest?"

"That Krannel can be seen means he's mortal. He's as threatened here as you are. More so. They'd have less hesitation about killing a dog. The wise course for you is to get away. Go through the forest and discover what lies on its far side. That kind of exploration is best done while you're young. And who knows, you might learn where your mother went."

Sudy's words revived a hope that Serollyn thought long dead, and she stopped resisting. After all, why stay in the midst of so many clan members who'd been false to the Life Lenders and had lied to the clan about having life-guides? She'd be happier somewhere else, though she dreaded having to pass through the forest.

The dream of finding her mother sustained Serollyn as they marched along the path winding between huge old trees. They each carried packs containing food, a light blanket of woven cotton, and changes of clothing. Serollyn had never ventured so far from their village, and while Marleon boasted that he had, she was certain that he exaggerated his ability to find his way.

No hunting party ever passed through this great forest to the land beyond it. The clanspeople knew little about the people who lived in the lands north of the forest—only what they learned from men who came from there in boats to trade iron pots and metal tools for lengths of brightly colored cotton cloth, wood carvings, palm oil, and woven baskets. The men from the north spoke the same language as the clans, though their accent was odd and their speech was sprinkled with unfamiliar words. Their dress was very different—no wraparounds, but garments they called trousers and shirts.

Serollyn thought it curious that these traders never stayed long or ventured far from their boats. They conducted their business quickly and returned to the sea, as though they found contact with the clans unsettling. Marleon told her that the clansmen who conducted the trade were unable to extract much information beyond the fact that the traders' people lived in "cities" and were ruled by "governors" and "magistrates" rather than a council of elders. Because the traders never spoke of having life-guides and gave no evidence of honoring the Life Lenders, the clan elders declared it taboo to travel beyond the forest.

And now they were breaking that taboo. That alone made Serollyn uncomfortable. If her mother had tried to pass through it, she had broken the taboo. And very likely had died in the attempt, much as Serollyn hoped otherwise. She could not forget that her father had been killed in this forest. She reminded herself that her father had not had a life-guide. If he had, he would have been protected. Possibly her mother's life-guide, her tern, had protected her.

Furthermore, Krannel had approved this expedition. She was safe with him. She replayed that thought over and over, convincing herself.

*It is well you are aware of the perils here.* Krannel's voice in her mind broke through her thoughts. *I will protect*

48

*you—all of you—as best I can, but I cannot foresee all dangers.*

*Are you speaking to all of us or only to me?* she thought back, not wanting Marleon and Nestryn to hear.

*Only to you.*

*Then tell me,* she begged, *you're leading us, aren't you? Marleon thinks he is, but you'll keep him from going the wrong way, won't you?*

*I'll do my best to keep you from going astray.*

She wanted to ask him more, but he ran ahead, barking furiously. They all halted, watching him, expecting some large beast or other menace. A dassie darted out from among the giant ferns and across the trail into the undergrowth on the other side, with Krannel chasing after the small creature, still barking.

*Whenever he doesn't want to answer, he puts on his dog act,* Serollyn thought.

*We have a long trek ahead,* Tolammy said, making Serollyn suspect he'd caught her thought even though she wasn't intending to send it. *We'll need meat. I think Krannel does not have great faith in your friend Marleon's ability as a hunter.*

Nestryn snickered and Marleon cast her a quizzical look. "Just something Tolammy said," Nestryn explained without explaining.

Krannel returned with a dassie hanging limply from his mouth. He placed it at Marleon's feet. *Clean it,* he said. *We can spare the time. It will be our supper.*

"Not much of a supper for three people," Marleon commented ungraciously. Serollyn guessed he would have preferred to hunt and catch the dassie himself.

Nestryn said, "It'll be enough. We can add wild herbs to make it taste better. I'll find some."

*Good,* Krannel said. *It is best to save what little we've brought for a time of greater need.*

Marleon removed the hunting knife he'd brought from its sheath and set to skinning and cleaning the small animal, spilling its blood onto the ground with the customary prayer of thanks to the Life Lenders.

"Our main need right now," Marleon said as he worked, "is to put as much distance between us and the clan as we can so we won't be found by a hunting party."

"Hunting us?" Serollyn asked.

"Hunting anything," he answered. "Even if they aren't looking for us and didn't know we'd gone, any hunters that find us will make us go back with them."

*Tolammy and I will know if there are hunters nearby,* Krannel assured him.

"It's so strange that Krannel can speak to all of us like that," Nestryn whispered to Serollyn.

"I know. I wish I knew how and why."

"Maybe that's what we're supposed to find out," Nestryn said.


With Krannel and Tolammy to guard them, Serollyn felt secure despite the discomfort of the shelter they'd found among the large, raised roots of a huge mahogany tree. Wrapped in the blanket she'd brought and cushioned on moss, she found her bed soft enough, but the roots offered no protection against the blood-sucking, biting insects that prowled over her. She kept swatting them and brushing them away even after Krannel assured her that none was poisonous. Despite the incessant trills of nightbirds, chirrs of insects, and croaks and calls of frogs, she finally fell asleep.

She awoke to someone shaking her shoulder. Startled, she sat upright. A hand covered her mouth before she could call out. "Shhh," Nestryn whispered in her ear. "Krannel told me to wake you. He heard the noise of someone crashing through the brush—a person, not an animal, he said. He's gone to investigate."

Serollyn opened her eyes. Dim light filtered through the trees. Dawn had come, but only recently.

"Where's Marleon?" she asked, looking around.

"Gone with Krannel," Nestryn said. "We're to wait here and stay quiet."

Tolammy sat on Nestryn's shoulder, and Serollyn found his presence comforting, certain that had he thought the danger great, he would have gone to confront it with Krannel and Marleon.

She straightened her wraparound, shook out and folded her blanket, and stuffed it into her backpack. Serollyn heard Krannel barking in the distance. At her urging, Nestryn helped gather up Marleon's belongings as well as their own. They concealed themselves and their packs behind the tree where they'd sheltered overnight.

Krannel's barking grew louder. *He's letting us know there's no danger,* Tolammy said.

"You might have told us that before we rushed so," Serollyn groused.

Tolammy yanked her braid.

"Ow!" She poked his shoulder. "Stop that!"

At that moment Krannel bounded into view, followed by Marleon, leading a limping Vali!

Serollyn ran to them. "Vali! What are you doing here?"

"Trying to find you," Vali said in a choked voice.

Her friend's eyes were red. She'd been crying.

"I thought I'd lost you. I've been wandering around all night. I was so scared, with no life-guide to protect me."

"Well, at least you finally admit you don't have one," Nestryn said as she joined them.

Serollyn, surprised by Nestryn's mean-spirited comment, asked, "Why've you been following us?"

"You're my closest friends," Vali said. "I wanted to be with you. And I was afraid."

"Afraid of what?" Nestryn asked.

"Of being found out, since you and Serollyn stirred everything up, and now, with the three of you gone, things will be even worse, with people suspicious of each other." Fresh tears flowed down her cheeks.

"So you want to go with us?" Serollyn asked, noting that through all of this talk Marleon remained silent, his expression unreadable.

"I don't really want to. I feel I have to," Vali said, wiping her face. "They've already accused me of lying about my life-guide."

"Who accused you?" Serollyn asked.

"Your grandmother. She said I should have gone with you because I lied, too."

"Sudy would never have said such a thing," Serollyn declared. "And what do you mean, you lied too? I didn't lie, and Sudy knows it."

"She did say it," Vali insisted, pouting. "And by 'too' she meant along with Marleon."

"She does know I lied," Marleon said slowly. "It could be true, Serollyn."

"Maybe. Do you want her to come with us?"

"Oh, please," Vali begged. "You have to let me. I'd never find my way back. I don't know the paths."

"You found your way to us," Nestryn pointed out, her voice sharp.

"I didn't. I was lost until your dog found me."

"He's my life-guide," Serollyn snapped.

"All right, your life-guide then."

"You want to come with us now, but what happens if you change your mind later?" Marleon said. "The way won't be easy, and you won't be able to go back."

"I won't change my mind," Vali said. "I promise."

*Should we let her?* Serollyn mindspoke to Krannel.

*Let Marleon decide,* came her life-guide's surprising answer. It seemed he spoke only to her; no one else gave any indication of having heard.

Marleon asked, "Serollyn? Nestryn? What do you think?"

"I say send her back," Nestryn said. "I don't mean to be cruel, Vali, but I know you so well. I don't think you're cut out for what lies ahead of us."

"But I don't know how to find my way back," Vali wailed. "You're my good friends. I want to be with you."

"Marleon, I think you should make the decision," Serollyn said.

He looked startled. Nestryn opened her mouth as if to object. Instead she nodded slowly. "I'll abide by whatever Marleon says. He knows this forest better than we do."

Serollyn doubted that. Nestryn came often to the forest to pick nuts and berries, and for all Marleon's great desire to be a hunter, he'd only accompanied a hunting party two or three times, and then only as a very junior member, primarily to check traps, not as a tracker.

Marleon looked decidedly uncomfortable about having the decision thrust on him. He shifted from foot to foot and cast glances at Krannel as if hoping the life-guide would come to his rescue. But Krannel remained silent.

Finally he said, "Vali, I think you made a great mistake in following us, and you're crazy to want to join us, but if you're determined, I guess you can come along."

Vali gave a little scream and threw her arms around Marleon's neck, hugging him. "Thank you. You won't be sorry." Adding, "Any of you," she went on to hug Nestryn and Serollyn as well. She even gave Krannel a pat on the head. He stepped away from her and did not wag his tail.

Vali didn't notice Krannel's coolness toward her, or maybe she simply did not care. Serollyn suspected that Vali still refused to believe that Krannel was anything more than a dog. But whatever her reason for coming had been, Vali went with them meekly enough, following Marleon's instructions without protest and being as friendly to Serollyn as if they had never argued.

As they penetrated more deeply into the forest, it became more difficult to find a trail. Hunters rarely ventured so far. The clan's hunting parties found sufficient game without going into the heart of the forest.

Marleon continued to lead the way, but he no longer made any attempt to conceal the fact that Krannel, trotting beside him, was finding the paths. With a turn of his head or a pointing of his nose, Krannel would indicate the direction they should go. Vali could have no idea that Krannel was also using mindspeech. Krannel confirmed that he never spoke in Vali's mind.

*Marleon must hear me not only to keep from getting us all lost but in case I need to warn of danger,* Serollyn's life-guide explained. *Vali has no such need and has not earned the right to be heard.*

Tolammy apparently agreed. Though he usually mindspoke privately to Nestryn, on occasion Serollyn and Marleon heard him as well, but Vali never did. Serollyn hoped that Vali did not know she was being excluded.

As they moved into the thickest part of the forest, food grew scarcer. Nuts, berries, and edible roots became less abundant than they had been during the early days of their trek. Krannel no longer caught dassies. The heavy canopy of leaves above them blotted out the sun, keeping the light dim and reducing the growth of underbrush. With little underbrush and no outcroppings of rock where dassies made their homes, they'd find no more of those small creatures. They rarely found berry bushes, and no nut-bearing trees grew in this part of the forest. They did find wild mushrooms, and Tolammy told them which were safe to eat. Wild boars rooted for the mushrooms, but although Krannel could frighten them away, they were too large for him to bring down. When Marleon wanted to try spearing one, the others talked him out of it, doubtful of his skill and too aware of the lethal rage of a wounded boar.

Water, at least, they had in abundance. They frequently encountered swift-running but narrow streams, easily forded. Rain fell often, and moisture dripped from the trees even when there was no rain. At night they huddled together, drawing warmth from each other through the cool, damp nights. Serollyn spread her poncho over them, but its inadequate cover grew even more inadequate as it became tattered from much use. Along with the rain, the noise of birds and frogs and large animals kept them awake. They grew weary and cross and wondered out loud when they would reach the end of the forest—and whether it had an end.

One night when Nestryn and Vali had fallen asleep, Serollyn snuggled against them, with Marleon lying beside her. She moved closer to him, trying to find a comfortable spot. He was awake, too, or perhaps her movement had awakened him. He drew her against him and whispered, "I'm sorry I got us all into this. But you're lucky to have Krannel. If only I really had a life-guide, this trek would be so much easier to bear."

She could think of no answer and so kept silent, hoping he would think she was asleep. Maybe he did. He whispered to Krannel, "Why did no life-guide come to me? What did I do wrong?"

Serollyn heard Krannel's reply clearly in her mind: *You decided beforehand that if no life-guide came to you, you would say one had come. Your great-cat was born in your mind. You named him Radic and imaged him so well that you left no space for your true guide.*

Marleon rolled away from her, and though she could see nothing, she guessed he'd sat up and inched nearer Krannel.

"You mean I would have received a guide if I hadn't planned to lie?" Marleon asked.

*I can't say what might have been. I can say that a great-cat does not easily or lightly serve as a life-guide.*

"I've confessed that I lied about Radic. If I put his image out of my thoughts, is there a chance I might get the life-guide meant for me?"

A new voice—Tolammy's—spoke. *You ask a question only the Life Lenders can answer. Walk carefully, hunt wisely, and let things happen as they may. You have been given the gift of hearing Krannel and me. Be content with that for now.*

Marleon said no more, but lay back down and threw

one arm across Serollyn's shoulders. She lay awake for some time thinking of what she had heard, and when at last she drifted off, she dreamed that she and Marleon were alone with Krannel in the forest and that Krannel told her he must now be life-guide for them both. And then he added, "Maybe I'll just be his from now on. You don't need me." Her scream of protest jolted her awake.

# 7

# WOOD BOYS

Footsore and tired, they sank down on a mossy hummock to rest. Serollyn guessed it wasn't much past midday, but it was hard to tell in this dark green world where they could see neither the sun by day nor the moons by night.

Vali sat next to Marleon and leaned against him. Serollyn wanted to do the same but refrained. Nestryn, her back against the trunk of a tree, picked idly at the moss, uprooting a bit of it and rolling it around in her palm. No one seemed to want to talk. Even Krannel and Tolammy seemed dispirited. Krannel lay quietly beside Serollyn, and Tolammy's shoulders slumped.

Krannel lifted his head and peered into the woods. Tolammy straightened and followed his gaze.

"What is it?" Serollyn asked.

"Don't know." Marleon pushed Vali away and rose to his feet. "Sounds like drumming."

"It couldn't be hunters, could it?" Nestryn asked, standing. "They wouldn't come this deep into the forest."

"They wouldn't be drumming if they did," Marleon said.

"Maybe we should hide from whatever it is," Serollyn said.

"It's been so long since we've seen anyone," Vali said plaintively. "If it's not hunters, let's see who it is."

"I'm not even sure where it's coming from." Marleon stepped off the hummock and stared into the forest. "Sound echoes so. I can't tell what direction to look in. Maybe Krannel can, or Tolammy."

Tolammy leaped from Nestryn's shoulder onto Krannel's back, and they trotted off through the trees.

"We'd better follow," Marleon said, helping Vali to her feet. Serollyn and Nestryn jumped up and started after their life-guides.

It was hard to keep the life-guides in sight and Serollyn was afraid of losing them. Krannel and Tolammy weren't communicating with them.

The drumming grew louder; they must be getting closer to its source. Serollyn wondered whether some animal might be making the sound, but there was a wild rhythm to the drumming that no animal could produce.

Her feet caught the rhythm; she found herself running, almost dancing. Nestryn did the same. Serollyn's weariness and discouragement fell away as she bounded into an unexpected clearing.

The drumming was loud here. The drummer must be nearby, but Serollyn's attention was drawn to the two boys who danced to the rapid rhythm of the drums.

Wild and unkempt, their chests bare, the boys capered about in ragged trousers so faded and worn that it was impossible to know what color they had been. Dirt smeared their clothes and skin as though they'd been rooting in the mud. Their dark hair had neither been combed nor cut for some time, perhaps never. But they sported toothy smiles and bright eyes and called out, "We dance. Come, join us. Dance to the drums like we do. Dance with us."

Without hesitating, without thinking, Serollyn ran into the clearing and began to dance. Nestryn followed. Moments later Marleon and Vali were gyrating alongside them. Krannel barked from the edge of the clearing, sharp angry barks, while Tolammy chittered and scolded, as monkeys will.

The dance became a romp. The two strange boys leaped and cavorted through and out of the clearing, leading the others in a frenzied chase.

What a chase it was, racing around trees, leaping over shrubs, balancing on fallen logs: a real follow-the-leader game filled with laughter.

The boys led the way back to the clearing, where they all collapsed on the ground, laughing and panting. Krannel and Tolammy remained on the edge of the clearing where they had stopped at the first sight of the boys. The drum had fallen silent.

Now the drumming started again, a different beat, slow but emphatic. The two dancing boys sat up and chanted in time to the beat, "What did you bring us? What did you bring us?"

"Who are you?" Nestryn asked, rising. "What do you want?"

"We are the wood boys," they chanted in unison. "We live in these woods. Tell us what you brought us. Tell us what you brought us."

"We have nothing," Serollyn said. "We weren't expecting to meet anyone here in the forest."

"They weren't expecting us," one said in time with the drumbeat.

"They've brought us nothing," the other chanted.

"That can't be!" they shouted, jumping to their feet and dancing around the clearing as the drum beat faster.

"They've brought a monkey and a dog," said one, pointing to Krannel and Tolammy.

"Monkeys are good eating," said the other, dancing near the two life-guides, who still did not move.

"Dogs are good for hunting," said the first.

They whirled and twirled away from the life-guides. One darted to Marleon, who was getting to his feet, and yanked from around Marleon's waist the wide cloth band that held his hunting knife and sheath along with a small woven bag that held flints for fire building. The boy waved the band triumphantly, and then tied it around his own waist and joined his companion in the wild dance, the knife in its sheath bouncing against his gyrating hips.

"We'll take the dog," sang out one.

"We'll take the monkey," intoned the second.

"We'll stew the monkey in the pot," they chanted.

"We'll eat his meat and suck his bones."

"The dog will get what's left."

"He'll hunt for us. He'll bring us meat."

"Stop!" Serollyn screamed. "Listen!"

The drumming ceased. An eerie silence filled the clearing. Not only had the drum and dancers fallen silent, but no one else spoke, and no sound of rustling leaves or trilling bird or chirring insect came from the forest. The world held its breath.

"Those are our life-guides," Serollyn said, her voice sounding unnaturally loud in the stillness. "I don't know how you can see the monkey, though everyone can see Krannel. But he *is* a life-guide. He's not a hunting dog.

And Tolammy is certainly not food."

One of the boys laughed. "Not food, she says."

"Life-guides, she says," chimed the other.

The drum beat a short, quick tattoo.

"We don't know what you mean," the two said together.

They broke again into dance, and the drum picked up the beat. They danced around Vali and Marleon, and Serollyn was shocked to see Vali join in the dance.

"They don't have life-guides," Serollyn whispered to Nestryn. "We've got to get away from here."

Nestryn nodded but did not move. Giving her an exasperated glare, Serollyn tried to evade the dancers to reach Krannel and Tolammy, who had not moved from their place at the edge of the clearing, though they must have heard the wood boys and must realize the danger.

Perhaps there was no danger. Perhaps the boys didn't actually intend harm; maybe this crazy dancing and chanting was all a game.

But she wanted to be at her life-guide's side in case trouble did erupt. As she snaked through the dance, she found her feet moving to the beat of the drum despite her efforts to resist. Marleon, too, joined the dance, while Nestryn still stood as though her feet had grown roots.

A wood boy linked arms with Serollyn. He smelled of dirt and rotting leaves, stale sweat, and carrion. Still she whirled around the clearing with him.

He handed her off to his partner, who was just as malodorous. She wove with him through the clearing, and when their path crossed that of Marleon and Vali, Serollyn caught hold of Marleon's arm and broke away from the wild boy, who grabbed Vali and spun away with her.

Gasping with relief and exertion, Serollyn said, "Help me. I've got to reach Krannel."

Marleon swung her toward the life-guides, their feet still moving to the drumbeats. As they danced near the clearing edge, Serollyn saw the wood boys dancing nearer. She had to reach Krannel before they reached her.

Marleon had a tight grip on her arm. She could not break away from him, so she pulled him with her as she lunged for Krannel.

The drum thundered. She couldn't think. But Krannel took a step closer to her, and she threw herself on him, her free arm circling his neck. Tolammy reached out and clutched Marleon's arm, so that the four of them were in contact, locked into a tight group embrace.

The drumming stopped, restarted—a slow, sinister throb. Serollyn felt it in her brain; she felt it in her blood. It did not make her want to dance; it made her want to die. Her body went limp, drained of energy, of will. Marleon loosed his hold on her, and she fell onto Krannel.

*Resist.* His voice shouted in her mind, overpowering the drum. She raised herself and grabbed Marleon. "Run!"

His dazed look told her he could not. And then the wild boys were on them, pulling them away from the life-guides, grabbing Krannel, catching hold of Tolammy.

Nestryn screamed and hurled herself at the boy whose hand had clamped around Tolammy's throat. Krannel, held by the scruff of his neck, let out a loud bark and sank his teeth into the arm of Tolammy's captor.

With a howl, the boy released Tolammy. The monkey leaped to Nestryn's shoulder, chittering furiously. Serollyn kicked hard at the boy who held Krannel. The boy's grip loosened, and Krannel tore himself free.

Serollyn caught Marleon's hand. "Run!" she repeated, and this time he did.

With Krannel dashing beside them, she and Marleon pounded into the forest, swerving around trees and leaping over roots. Nestryn and Tolammy ran so close behind that Nestryn trod on Serollyn's heels.

They ran and dodged and ducked and raced, until the sounds grew fainter, and the noise of the drum faded. When they could run no farther, they collapsed in a fortress of tree roots, huddled together, panting. Nestryn hugged Tolammy in a tight embrace. Serollyn rested her head on Krannel and stroked him. Marleon slid his arms around her waist. His body trembled—or was it her own?

Nestryn was the first to recover. She jerked upright, still holding Tolammy against her breast. "Vali!"

"Vali," Serollyn echoed. "She didn't come with us."

"What'll they do to her?" Nestryn asked, shuddering.

"We can't leave her back there," Serollyn said. "We have to go get her."

"You and Nestryn stay here," Marleon said. "I'll go."

"By yourself? Marleon, don't be silly."

*I'll go with him,* Krannel said.

"Without me?" Serollyn demanded, her hand tightening on Krannel's back.

"The risk to you and Nestryn is too great. Stay here and let Tolammy guard you. Krannel and I can rescue Vali."

"You'd endanger your life and my life-guide for her?"

"She's our age-mate and our friend. We can't just abandon her," Marleon said. "And we were running blindly when we ran away. I need Krannel to help find the way."

"Tolammy could lead you," Serollyn said impulsively.

"I can't see Tolammy," Marleon reminded her. "It has to be Krannel."

"But I'm afraid of losing him!"

Krannel growled and snapped.

"You're wasting time arguing while Vali's life is in danger," Nestryn said.

"Oh, all right," Serollyn conceded. "I'll trust the Life Lenders to take care of you both—and of Vali. But Krannel, please, tell me what you're doing."

*If I can, I will,* was all the promise she got.

She watched as Marleon stood and left the shelter of the roots, Krannel trotting along beside him.

*Please, bring them both back safely to me,* Serollyn prayed silently.

# 8

# ANTS

Serollyn waited anxiously with Nestryn, remembering the dream she'd had, now come to terrifying reality with Krannel leaving her to go off with Marleon.

She knew Marleon needed Krannel to guide him to the wood boys. And to keep him safe and bring him and Vali back safely. But she thought of how Krannel had stood like a woodcarving on the edge of the clearing, as though he could not move to help her while the drums sounded.

She wanted to ask Tolammy about that but was afraid of the answer she might hear. Perhaps she should not worry Nestryn needlessly. But Nestryn had her life-guide here with her, while Serollyn's life-guide was risking his life. And Marleon had gone into danger. All to rescue foolish Vali who was a burden on them, while without Marleon and Krannel they would be hopelessly lost.

If she had gone with them—if they had all gone back for Vali, she would not feel so conflicted. Why did she hear nothing from Krannel?

*They have almost reached the clearing,* Tolammy mindspoke. *Krannel will report what he can to me, and I will relay it to you both. It requires less of his energy that way.*

"Is the drumming still going on?" Serollyn asked. "Are the wood boys still there?"

Tolammy did not answer. "He can only tell us what Krannel tells him," Nestryn reminded her. "Try to be patient."

Serollyn tried to distract herself. "What do you think the wood boys are? They're so odd!"

"I've been wondering about that, too," Nestryn said. "Under all that dirt they aren't different in appearance from us. It's their behavior that makes them so peculiar. I wonder, since you didn't see any life-guides with them, if they could be children of clan members who wandered into the woods when they failed to get life-guides?"

Serollyn thought about it. "No, they didn't have any," she said. "But that drumming was so strange. It made us dance. Why couldn't we resist it?"

*The clearing is empty,* Tolammy reported, interrupting their speculation. *They've gone off somewhere with Vali. Krannel is following the trail.*

"I don't like the sound of that," Serollyn said. "I think we should go after them."

"They told us to wait here."

"But who knows where and how far the wood boys have gone. Tolammy, couldn't you could find their trail?"

*I could, but Krannel and Marleon wanted you to stay out of danger.*

"It isn't right for us to be safe while they're risking their lives," Serollyn objected.

*The more of us there are following the wood boys, the greater the danger will be.*

"Do *you* know who the boys are, Tolammy? Or what they are?" Nestryn asked. "Are they human?"

*They are human,* the life-guide replied. *Though they call themselves "wood boys," the name is inaccurate. They neither come from the forest nor belong to it. They do harm to it. The forest does not want them here.*

"How do you know that?" Nestryn asked.

*I feel the forest's pain,* Tolammy said. *I sense the anger of all the forest creatures at the boys' presence. And especially at the drummer's.*

It grew late; night came early to the forest. Nestryn and Tolammy gathered what dry sticks they could find near their shelter and built a small fire. They huddled near it as much for the comfort of seeing each other as for the bit of warmth it provided.

Tolammy had received no further messages from Krannel, and Serollyn was growing frantic. "They must be in trouble," she said. "We have to go after them."

*Wait! Krannel is trying to send me a message, but something is interfering—the drums, I think.*

Serollyn heard them, then. Faint, from a great distance, came their rapid beat. She jumped up. "We can follow the sound," she said. "Even if you won't take us, Tolammy, we can follow the sound."

*No!* In his agitation, Tolammy chittered frantically, leaped from Nestryn's shoulder to Serollyn's, yanked her braid, and jumped back to Nestryn.

"Tolammy understands more about this than we do, Serollyn. We'd better do as he says."

"But it's not your life-guide who's in danger."

"No, but it's my friends as well as yours. I—"

*They're coming,* Tolammy interrupted. *They have Vali. The wood boys are after them. Get ready.*

Serollyn looked around for something to use as a

weapon but saw only a fallen branch too rotten to do any damage. She picked it up anyway.

The drums still sounded far away, but she had no sooner picked up the branch than Marleon came into view, Vali slung over his shoulders. Nestryn ran forward and helped him lower Vali to the ground.

The two wood boys came charging after them, whooping and shouting. Krannel ran along beside them, barking and snapping at their legs. Swinging the branch, Serollyn jumped in front of Marleon, Vali, and Nestryn. The wood boys dashed toward her, their stench gagging her. She hurled the branch at them.

As she'd feared, it broke in pieces when it struck, too soft to do any harm. It did not stop them, but as they launched themselves at Marleon, one cried out and the other joined in. Instead of grabbing Marleon, they clawed at their chests where the branch had struck.

Marleon grabbed one and threw him to the ground, and with Krannel's help Serollyn toppled the other. Instead of rising and fighting, the two wood boys rolled on the ground, beating their chests and slapping their faces as though they were on fire. Marleon seized the opportunity to unfasten his knife belt and pull it away from its writhing wearer. Seconds later Marleon, too, was slapping at his arms.

Serollyn felt something crawling on her arm, and a sharp sting brought burning pain. The branch that she'd thought useless must have been full of stinging insects, probably fierce ants of the type the clan called marauders for their vicious attacks. Though the firelight was not bright enough to see them, dozens of ants must have landed on the wood boys. And in removing the knife belt,

Marleon had also acquired some of the stinging insects.

"Are you all right?" Serollyn called out to him.

"Marauder ants," he called back. "I've been stung, but I think I got them all off me." He shook his knife belt, examined it carefully, and put it on.

The wood boys were still screaming and writhing so that Nestryn and Marleon grabbed Vali up out of the way barely in time to keep them from rolling onto her.

*We must go.*

Nestryn and Marleon must have heard Krannel's mental warning along with Serollyn. All three of them, with Tolammy and Krannel, scrambled away from the screaming wood boys, Marleon and Nestryn carrying Vali between them. Marleon panted with exhaustion.

"Let me take her," Serollyn said, shifting Vali's arm from Marleon's shoulder to hers.

Relieved of that burden, Marleon fell back behind them, while Krannel led them through the darkness. His leading and Tolammy's guidance did not keep them from blundering into trees and stumbling over roots.

"We can't go far like this," Marleon said.

But at that instant crashes and cries came from behind them, and they barely had time to squeeze aside when the wood boys ran past them. Moments later loud splashes told them the boys had jumped into a stream to ease their stings and shake off the ants.

"That'll be the first bath they've had in a good long while," Marleon said with a chuckle.

"Then we did them a favor," Serollyn agreed. "They needed a bath."

"But they'll be angrier than ever," Nestryn put in. "We need to get away from them."

"No," Marleon said. "What we need to do, now that they're temporarily helpless, is to go back to their lair, overpower the drummer, and destroy the drums. Krannel says the drummer uses the drums to control them."

"Are you crazy, Marleon? You're worn out, Vali needs care, and it's too dark to see where we're going."

"I know it's a lot to ask, but if we don't act now, while we have the advantage, we'll continue to be in danger from them," Marleon said.

*He's right*, Krannel put in. *And we have a better chance in the dark. Tolammy and I can guide you to the lair. But we do have to act fast.*

"How can we do that, having to carry Vali?" Nestryn protested. "Marleon needs to rest, and so do we."

*We'll get little rest if we don't do it*, Tolammy said, swinging onto Krannel's back.

The life-guide's logic persuaded her. "All right, let's get started," Serollyn said.

# 9

# BATTLE

Vali regained consciousness as they made their way through the dark night. "Where …? How …?"

"We got you away from the wood boys," Marleon said. "You're safe."

*Safe? Are any of us safe?* Serollyn wondered.

*In comparison to the condition from which we rescued her, she is safe,* Krannel mindspoke. *They had her tied to a stake ready to be cooked and eaten.*

"How horrible!" In her shock Serollyn spoke aloud. "What monsters would do such a thing?"

"Now you understand why we have to stop them," Marleon said.

"But how is destroying the drums going to help?" Nestryn asked.

*Tell me something,* Krannel said. *Did you see the drummer? What did he look like?*

Serollyn admitted she'd seen nothing more than a blur.

"I didn't see him," Marleon said. "He was in a kind of burrow—with his drums."

"You aren't making any sense," Vali said crossly. "What are you talking about?"

"They're talking to Serollyn's life-guide," Nestryn explained. "Do you think you can walk a little? We could move faster if we weren't carrying you."

"I can try," she said, scrunching her face in a grimace of pain Serollyn suspected was exaggerated for their benefit.

Serollyn was glad to be relieved of Vali's weight, which she and Nestryn had been sharing. Now she only had to offer Vali an arm to lean on.

"Where is this lair we're heading for?" Serollyn asked. "And what is it?"

"It's a hut made of piles of brush and tree limbs in a burned-out area," Marleon said. "It looks like a swamp rat's nest, but it's on dry ground. And it smells worse than any rat's nest."

*Quiet! No more talking,* Krannel sent. *We're almost there.*

"Why are we going there?" Vali wailed, apparently just comprehending their intended destination.

"Shhh!" Serollyn hissed. "Krannel says we have to be quiet."

Vali tried to protest, but at her first word Nestryn clamped a hand over her mouth. They entered a clearing above which Krissa, the larger moon, three-quarters full, was near enough to zenith to give a bit of light, enough to make out what looked like a pile of sticks and branches in the center of the clearing.

*That's the lair,* Krannel said, confirming what Serollyn had guessed. *The entrance is on the other side.*

Proceeding slowly and quietly, they circled the odd shelter until they saw a dark opening in the mound of sticks. They neared the opening, but stopped at the sound of a low, soft drumbeat.

Serollyn peered into the opening, smelled a foul stench, but couldn't see the drummer. Vali, though, gave a surprised cry. "It's Veral," she said. "It must be."

"Hush!" Nestryn hissed. "Don't be silly."

But Vali rushed forward, crying "Veral! You've come to me. They can't see you, but I can."

"She's gone mad!" Marleon said and headed after her.

*She is not mad, only mistaken,* Krannel mindspoke. *She sees what she has always pictured as her life-guide. But what she sees is not sent by the Life Lenders.*

Tolammy added, *You will not find it easy to convince her that what she sees is a thing of evil, but you must if you are to save her.*

Marleon grabbed Vali and tried to pull her back, but she fought him, kicking, twisting, and biting until he was forced to release her. Immediately she ducked back inside.

*You must destroy the drums,* Krannel instructed. *When you do that, it will be easier to deal with Vali.*

Serollyn moved toward the doorway, and Nestryn followed close behind, her hand clutching Serollyn's wraparound. Ahead, Marleon kept his hand on the hilt of his knife but did not draw it from its sheath. As he tried to reach the drums, Vali shouted. "Don't come any closer," pushing and jabbing at him to keep him from passing her.

Try as she might, Serollyn could see nothing beyond Marleon and Vali inside the shelter. They were blocking her view, and even outside the light was dim. While Marleon wrestled with Vali, Serollyn tried to slip around them. Krannel helped by nipping Vali's legs, keeping her off balance and too busy to interfere with Serollyn.

The shelter was as rough inside as out. Serollyn's wraparound caught on twigs and she nearly lost it. She had to disentangle it and rewrap it while being jostled by Marleon and Vali. Finally she got in behind them, but could see nothing.

*Krannel, Tolammy, I can't see him. Where is he? Where are the drums?*

At the same moment that Krannel said, *In front of you,* a small, taloned hand closed around her wrist. She could not break the bruising grip.

"Nestryn, he's got hold of me!" She pried at the fingers.

Tolammy leaped from Nestryn's shoulder onto Serollyn's, made another leap, and clawed and beat at whatever held her. *Nestryn, grab the drums,* he sent.

Nestryn groped past Serollyn. "I can't find them."

Still struggling to free herself, Serollyn felt around for the drums. But her arms were being scratched and gouged in the fight between Tolammy and the drummer; she was being bumped and bruised in the battle between Marleon and Vali; and the drummer, whatever it was, gripped her wrist so tightly that her hand grew numb.

*It's hopeless,* she sent. *I can't find any drums, and I can't breathe, and I'm getting beat up.*

*Work your way out,* Krannel sent. *I have another plan.*

Work her way out! How could she, with no room to move and the drummer-thing clamped onto her arm, and Tolammy still fighting it, and Nestryn trying to help him?

But Nestryn and Marleon must have heard Krannel's message just as she had, and they all somehow backed out of the place little by little as they fought.

When she stumbled through the opening and regained the clearing, Serollyn took deep breaths of the cool air that, while not free of the sickening odor of the lair, was at least an improvement.

Whatever it was that had hold of her wrist was visible in the faint moonlight only as a blot of darkness. She might have thought it only a shadow, had she not seen Tolammy battling that dark blot.

Suddenly the grip on her wrist released, Tolammy leaped onto Nestryn's shoulder, chittering wildly, and Vali let out a delighted cry.

"You've come to me, Veral," she said. "Help me!"

Marleon backed away from Vali and groped in the bag on his belt. He got out flints, struck them, and sent sparks into the pile of sticks that formed the wood boys' refuge. The dry branches caught fire easily. Flames roared up.

"No!" Vali howled. "Veral says you mustn't."

She tried to reach the burning lair, but Marleon and Nestryn together grabbed her and held her back, while Krannel, barking furiously, blocked the way.

*Get back!* Krannel ordered, as sparks flew from the fire, threatening their hair and flesh.

They had to drag Vali from the clearing. As they approached the edge, Marleon gave her a hard shove that sent her stumbling into the woods. They kept going, pulling Vali along with them, until they were a safe distance from the blaze.

"Is that thing still with us?" Nestryn asked when they stopped.

"That *thing* is my life-guide," Vali said. "I don't understand why you tried to kill him. And yes, he's on my shoulder. You mean the all-seeing Serollyn can't see him?"

"It's too dark to see anything," Serollyn said, not wanting to reveal that even in the moonlit clearing she saw only a black shadow.

"And you can't hear him when he speaks to me?" Vali

asked. "You can hear each other's life-guides, but you can't hear mine? Good."

No one had answered her question, but it must have been obvious to her that they could not hear.

*Is that really Veral?* Serollyn asked Krannel, whom she heard noisily licking his wounds.

*He's a Sneak, a creature of the Death Stealers,* her life-guide replied. *He'll let her call him anything she wants.*

*We have to get rid of him!* Nestryn said. *He'll destroy her!*

*She's safe for the moment. Tolammy and I will work on a plan to protect us all, but right now we need to rest. We'll have to put up with him until morning.*

*But do we dare wait until then?* Serollyn asked.

*Can he hear your mindspeech?* Nestryn wondered.

*He can't hear ours just as we can't hear his,* Tolammy answered.

*It would be more dangerous to try to do something now, in the darkness, with everyone exhausted,* Krannel advised Serollyn. *Tolammy and I will keep watch to be certain he doesn't persuade Vali to go off with him while you sleep.*

The life-guides led them to a kapok tree with wall-like roots that offered them some protection but no comfort beyond what they got from closeness to each other.

Vali slept apart from the others. The space they were crowded into did not permit her to get very far away, but she got as close to the sheltering root as she could and kept her back turned to the rest.

"Do you think Vali will get over this conviction that that thing is her life-guide?" Marleon whispered as he, Serollyn, and Nestryn lay bundled together between Krannel and Tolammy.

"She must," Serollyn said.

*It will not be easy to convince her,* Krannel mindspoke to them all. *It is unfortunate that the evil creature has taken a form so like her invented life-guide.*

"That's not a coincidence, is it?" Marleon asked.

*I do not think it is a coincidence,* Tolammy answered. *I suspect it purposely appeared to her in that form.*

And Krannel said, *The Sneak is sent by the Death Stealers to cause discord and strife leading to violent death. So long as Vali clings to it, we are all in danger.*

*But we can do nothing tonight,* Tolammy said. *You must sleep while you can. Krannel and I will keep guard.*

Worn out as they all were, they had no trouble taking that advice.

# 10

# STRIFE

Before she knew it, Serollyn awoke from a disturbing dream to find daylight filtering greenly through the leaves above her. The dream fled from her memory as soon as she sat up, but the disquiet lingered.

Having nothing to breakfast on, they needed very little time to get ready to journey. The narrow space between the trees forced them to walk single file. Krannel led the way, with Marleon following directly behind him. Vali walked after Marleon, head held high, deigning to speak to no one but the thing she alone could see. Nestryn followed Vali, Tolammy perched on her shoulder.

Angry at being relegated to the end of the procession and separated from Krannel, who again seemed to prefer Marleon's company to hers, Serollyn shouted, "Are we heading any place in particular? Or are we just wandering in circles in this endless forest?"

"Your life-guide is leading us. Doesn't he know what he's doing?" Nestryn called back, not turning her head.

"Life-guide!" Vali snorted. "That stupid dog, a life-guide? We know better, don't we, Veral?"

Whatever answer "Veral" gave sent her into gales of harsh laughter. Infuriated, Serollyn lunged at Vali and shoved her forward, into Nestryn. Nestryn whirled around, struck out at Vali, and yanked her hair.

"Ow!" Vali raked her fingernails across Nestryn's cheek. With a curse Marleon grabbed Nestryn's shoulders and jerked her back against him. Vali leaped onto both of them, clawing and screaming. Serollyn hurled herself onto Vali, pounding her fists against Vali's back.

Vali lashed out with blows and kicks. The others fought back, striking out indiscriminately. Soon Serollyn no longer knew nor cared who was hitting whom, or why. She only wanted to hurt someone. Anyone. The others must have felt the same. She was pummeled from every direction.

*Stop! Hold off!* Krannel's call thundered into her mind, stunning her. *Look!*

She froze. His command was deafening. She gazed around in confusion, saw Tolammy hanging by one hand from a high branch, swinging wildly, his other hand clawing at an invisible opponent. Vali grabbed for him, but he was just out of her reach.

No. Vali couldn't see Tolammy. She must be grabbing for his opponent. The Sneak. Nestryn pushed Vali aside to try to help Tolammy. Krannel leaped up, snarling and snapping, but his jumps fell short.

Marleon had his knife out. Unable to see the fighters, he could only grab Vali and keep her out of the fray by threatening her with the knife.

Blood streamed from Tolammy's shoulder where a chunk had been torn from it. His face was bleeding, covered with scratches. And his head was bending back, his neck twisting in what had to be a death grip by his opponent.

Nestryn, hysterical, clutched Marleon's arm. "Do something!" she pled.

"How?" he snapped, shrugging free of her hold. "I can't see anything but a moving branch. What can I do?"

That branch, from which Tolammy hung, bobbed and shook with the violence of the battle.

"He's hurting Veral," Vali shouted. "Make him stop!"

Serollyn ground her teeth in fury, though she knew that Vali couldn't see Tolammy, couldn't know that Veral was winning the fight.

Tolammy lost his grip and hurtled toward the ground. Krannel dived beneath him, breaking his fall. But Tolammy rolled off him onto the ground. The monkey was gasping, his tongue protruding from his mouth, his neck twisted. Serollyn screamed. The Sneak must be on top of him, choking him.

Krannel crouched beside him, trying to sink his teeth into the unseen foe. Nestryn threw herself on the ground and tried to yank Tolammy free, but his head only bent more, until Serollyn was afraid his spine would crack.

Marleon pushed Vali aside and ran to Krannel. His knife drawn, he knelt beside Krannel. Vali followed and grabbed his shoulders, trying to pull him away. His knife plunged toward Tolammy. But the blade encountered something before it reached the monkey. It stopped, its point just above Tolammy's chest.

Nestryn slid Tolammy from beneath the knife and caught him up in her arms, hugged his limp form to her breast.

Vali screamed and beat on Marleon with her fists. "You've killed him," she screeched. "You've killed Veral."

Marleon straightened, still gripping the knife, and

stared at the blood dripping from its blade. Vali left off pounding Marleon and bent, gathered something into her arms, and cradled it as a child cradles an imaginary doll. But the blood that soaked her chest and arms was real.

For some time they stood motionless, Marleon staring at his knife, Vali hunched over the unseen Sneak, Nestryn seated on the ground with Tolammy on her lap. Serollyn stood beside Krannel, feeling befuddled and helpless. And also very ashamed. She'd lost her temper and fought with her friends. And they'd all fought back. Not just Vali—all of them.

They were all tired and overwrought, but that didn't excuse them. They all understood the importance of working together, of depending on one another. Yet they'd all just fallen apart at the same time, it seemed.

*It was the Sneak, sowing discord among you,* Krannel sent, consoling her.

"He's dead." Vali's voice was leaden with despair. "You killed my life-guide."

"I'm sorry," Serollyn said, and, not being truly sorry, could think of nothing more to say. *Is he dead?* she sent to Krannel. *Can he die?*

Krannel trotted to her side. *Not in the sense that people die,* he responded. *We are rid of him for the present. He may appear again later in another form.*

Serollyn looked at Tolammy, still cradled in Nestryn's arms. *What about Tolammy?* she asked. *Is he—can he be dead?* He seemed so small and helpless, his breathing ragged, his eyes closed.

*He could have died,* her life guide replied. *We are not immortal, though we can sometimes come back from death just as the Death Stealers' creature can. But Marleon stopped the Sneak in time to prevent Tolammy's death. He is injured, but he will recover.*

"Krannel says he'll recover," Serollyn said, not certain that Nestryn and Marleon had heard.

"He was so brave," Nestryn said, and tears rolled down her cheeks. "Why did that thing attack him?"

*The Death Stealers are enemies of life-guides,* Krannel explained. *They steal lives given by the Life Lenders. Our aim is to preserve life. If the Sneak had succeeded in killing Tolammy or even leaving him gravely wounded, he could then have more easily caused one or more of you to suffer an untimely and violent death.*

"Tolammy *has* been gravely wounded," Nestryn said, smoothing the monkey's brow. "Thank the Life Lenders-- and thank you--for showing Marleon how to kill that thing."

*Remember what I told you: he cannot be permanently killed. We must hope Tolammy recovers completely before he returns.*

In the distance a great-cat howled.

# 11

# NAMES

After their ordeal, none of them could face the prospect of resuming their trek. They all needed rest. Nestryn held Tolammy and stroked him. Vali stood apart, still cradling the thing she believed to have been her life-guide, not speaking but glowering at them all. Serollyn could think of no way to convince Vali that the creature Marleon killed had not been a life-guide. She slipped into awkward silence, a torpor born of helplessness.

A crashing behind them jolted her from her lethargy. She turned and shouted an alarm. The two wood boys stumbled from between trees. They ran to Vali.

She looked up. "Veral said you'd come, but you're too late." She lowered her gaze to the thing in her arms.

The wood boys must have seen what she held. "The drummer can't be dead," one said, horror filling his voice.

The wood boys' faces were red and swollen from the ant bites, and they'd smeared their bare chests with mud, now spotted with blood where they'd scratched the bites. One was limping badly. They kept their eyes fixed on Vali.

"Help us," one said. The plea might have been addressed to Vali or to the slain drummer.

"We're lost and we hurt," the other chimed in.

They reminded Serollyn of small children; she pitied them, especially when Vali turned away from them and lost herself again in grief over the dead thing in her arms. She went to stand next to them. "I'm sorry you're hurt."

"You hurt us," one said.

"You were going to kill our friend," Serollyn said.

"You took her away from us," the other boy said.

"You burned the drums," said the first.

"And now you've killed our drummer," the second said.

*Talk to them. Keep them distracted,* Krannel advised.

"He would have killed one of us," Serollyn said. "We don't wish anyone's death."

While they talked, Marleon had slipped into the trees. Serollyn saw him emerge and grab one of the boys. She darted forward, shoved the other boy away, and caught hold of the arm of the other.

The boy Serollyn had seized let out an agonized howl. She released her hold. He hid behind Vali and licked the arm, whimpering.

Marleon held on to the boy he'd grabbed until that one let out a series of eerie howls that made Marleon release him and back away from him.

*I think they're in pain from the ant bites, and your touch irritated the bites and also frightened them,* Krannel sent.

"I can find something to put on your bites to keep them from stinging," Nestryn said, easing Tolammy to the ground beside her. "There are leaves I can mash into a healing paste, if you'll trust me to get them and put the paste on you."

"I'll get the plants," Serollyn said. "You shouldn't leave Tolammy."

"No, it's all right. He told me to go. I know better than you what to look for and where to look."

Serollyn hadn't heard Tolammy's mind speech, nor did he look conscious. But when she would have objected, Krannel said, *She's right. Let her go. You are needed here.*

*I can see Tolammy, but I can't care for him like Nestryn,* she sent dubiously. *And Marleon can't see him.*

*Tolammy doesn't need your care. He only needs rest. You must look after the wood boys.*

Marleon stepped up beside Serollyn. "What do we do?" he asked. "They seem so harmless and helpless. I think I could overpower them easily enough, but then what?"

"I think they *are* helpless now that the drummer's dead," Serollyn said. "So what do we do with them?"

The boys, who looked only a year or two younger than she and her friends, acted like younglings not yet ready for schooling. Thinking of Marleon's youngest brothers and sisters, whom she had often helped care for, she could not help feeling they needed her protection. *Krannel,* she sent, *are the boys still a danger to us?*

*Only if their fear gains control over them. You must prevent that from happening.*

"How can we do that?" Marleon asked.

*I cannot say. You must find the way.*

At that unhelpful answer, Marleon looked questioningly at Serollyn.

She shrugged. "We'd better try to win their confidence."

Serollyn went to the weeping boy. "We won't hurt you," she said quickly, noting his look of panic. "Our friend will be back soon with the healing paste. What are your names?"

The boy glanced at Vali, his gaze fixed not on her face but on what she held in her arms. *"He* called us Fear and Dread. I'm Fear."

Marleon came up beside her. "That can't be your real name," he said.

The boy flinched as though Marleon had struck him and ducked behind Serollyn as though he expected another blow.

"My name is Serollyn, and he's Marleon. Those are real names. Fear and Dread aren't."

The boy hung his head and shifted from foot to foot. "They're all the names we got," he said.

"If Veral gave them those names, you've no right to criticize them," Vali said, startling Serollyn, who'd been so focused on calming the boy who called himself Fear and getting more information that she'd almost forgotten Vali's presence.

"We're Fear and Dread," the boy said, slipping back into the singsong they'd used previously.

"We're Dread and Fear," the other said, the one with the limp.

"The Drummer named us, and the Drummer cared for us," the two said in unison.

*We're losing ground,* Serollyn sent.

Marleon clamped a hand on Vali's shoulder and drew her back, away from the boys. "We want to help them," he said. "You're upsetting them."

Vali twisted in Marleon's grip.

Serollyn carefully took the boys' hands in her own and drew them away from Vali and Marleon. "Are you hungry?" she asked them. "We have a little food."

Dread ignored her, keeping his gaze fixed on Vali, but

Fear licked his lips and mumbled, "Hungry."

"Come on, then." She led them to a mossy knoll, removed her backpack, and took out the last of the dried fish. She was glad for Krannel's foresight in insisting they save it for a time of need and live off what the forest provided as long as they could.

She offered Fear the first piece. He took it and crammed most of it into his mouth.

"Be careful," she warned. "There may be bones."

But he paid her no heed and devoured it so fast she doubted he'd even tasted it.

Dread watched his companion and slowly reached for the piece Serollyn held out to him. He accepted it gingerly, broke off a small piece, and nibbled at it, as though afraid it would poison him.

*Well, at least there's* some *difference between them,* Serollyn thought with satisfaction. *They don't always act exactly alike.*

She heard steps and looked up to see Nestryn approach with a handful of leaves. "I had to hunt farther than I'd expected," she said. "I'm going to mash them into a paste, but in the meantime I found a stream where they can wash off that mud. They'll need to be clean before I can put the paste on them."

Dread dropped his piece of fish and jumped back. "We don't like to wash," he said.

Fear grabbed up the dropped fish and jammed it into his mouth, while Serollyn caught Dread by the arm.

Again she hurt him without meaning to, and again he let out a loud howl that brought Vali running to him. She no longer carried with her the body of the Death Stealers' Sneak, but what she'd done with it, Serollyn had no idea.

"He doesn't want to wash, but he has to," Serollyn explained.

Marleon came up behind Vali. "Let them be," he told her. "They're trying to help the boys."

She scowled. "You should leave them alone. They don't need the kind of help Nestryn's trying to give."

"But Nestryn knows what she's doing. You know she does." He tried to draw her away.

She turned on him screaming, her eyes wild. "I'm going home," she shouted. "I'll tell them all what you did. How you killed a life-guide."

"He wasn't a life-guide, and he nearly killed Tolammy," Nestryn called back.

"You'll get lost," Marleon said. "You'll never find your way home."

But there was no reasoning with Vali. When Marleon tried to approach her, she turned and ran. When he would have run after her, Krannel said, *Let her go. In her state of mind she endangers us all. She's capable of killing. You'd have to watch her every moment.*

"Yes, let her go," Nestryn agreed bitterly. "She wanted Tolammy to die."

No one went after Vali. She vanished into the forest.

With Vali gone, Nestryn persuaded Fear to go with her to the stream. Dread refused to go along, so Serollyn stayed with him and attempted to reassure him.

"Your friend won't be hurt," she said quietly. "She'll stop the bites from itching and burning. When you see how much better he feels, you'll want to let her help you."

She hoped that would be true. She couldn't drag Dread to the stream and didn't want to frighten him more. With Vali gone, Serollyn hoped they could win the boys over.

They were making good progress with Fear.

And those names! Fear and Dread were terrible names; the Sneak must have bestowed them to bind the boys to the Death Stealers. She had a sudden inspiration.

"I know 'Dread' can't be your real name, and since you don't know any other, I'm going to give you a new name. I'm going to call you Dedryc."

He blinked and stared as if unable to comprehend.

"Dedryc is a good name," she said. "It means leader."

"Dedryc," he repeated, and again, "Dedryc," as though rolling the name about on his tongue, tasting it. His lips curved slowly into a smile.

"How did you hurt your foot?"

"Stepped on a sharp stick," he said, lifting his foot to display a nasty wound.

"Nestryn can clean and bandage it for you, and that will make it feel better. You'll have to come with me to the stream. We'll see how your friend is doing. I'll call him Feryn. That's a much better name than 'Fear.'"

Taking a gentle hold on his elbow, she steered him to the stream, where they found Nestryn already smearing the paste she'd made onto her charge's chest. She looked up and grinned. "Looks a lot cleaner, doesn't he?"

"He looks like a new person," Serollyn said. "And I have a new name for him. Feryn. How does that sound?"

"I like it," Nestryn said. "It's a good name."

"What does it mean?" Dedryc asked.

"Far-reacher," Serollyn said. "It is a name of honor among our people. Do you like the name?"

"Ye-e-e-s," Feryn said, the word drawn out thoughtfully. And then definitely, "Yes. I like Feryn better."

"Then Feryn is your name. And Dedryc is his name."

Hearing the name, Dedryc, whom Nestryn was leading into the stream, grinned and waved at Feryn, then stood docilely, letting Nestryn lave water onto his chest and use moss to sponge off the mud.

"Now we'll have to get you some clean clothes," Serollyn told Feryn. "You can't put on those filthy, torn rags. We'll show you how to wear wraparounds and give you a couple of our extra ones."

While Nestryn ministered to Dedryc, caring for his foot and for the ant bites, Feryn ran about in the nude to dry off. Serollyn fetched her pack and took out one of her two spare wraparounds. She showed Feryn how to wind it around him and tuck it securely. He strutted about, quite pleased with the brightly colored garment.

When Nestryn finished caring for Dedryc, Marleon took his one extra wraparound from his pack and gave it to Nestryn so she could get it on Dedryc. He bent over the stream, admiring his reflection.

The boys were acting almost normal, free of the evil influence of the drummer. Now she had the responsibility of keeping them free.

# 12

# HUNTERS

With their numbers increased, Serollyn knew even before Krannel pointed it out that they would need to replenish their supply of food. Game could be found with some effort. An occasional moon rat scooted across their path, and springers could be heard leaping through the brush in the distance. Krannel could bring down a fairly large animal, and Marleon was more than willing to use his hunting skills. They disliked the idea of leaving the others to hunt. Krannel offered to scout for game while Marleon remained behind. But Marleon insisted on going, and Serollyn and Nestryn assured him that they could handle Feryn and Dedryc, now that Vali was gone.

Serollyn wondered how Vali would find food and what would keep her safe from the beasts that prowled by night. But Vali had chosen her path, no matter how difficult. Serollyn thrust aside her concern to question Feryn and Dedryc. She wanted to learn all she could from them, now that Vali and the messenger of the Death Dealers were gone.

"You called yourselves 'wood boys,' but I don't believe you're any more a part of these woods than we are," she said, thinking that they were even less a part. They lacked the woods lore of her and her friends. "Where did you live before you came into the woods and why did you come here?"

The two boys gazed at each other as though each hoped the other might answer. Finally Dedryc shrugged. "Don't know," he said.

"Don't remember," Feryn added.

"You don't recall anything about your life before you were in this forest?"

Again they looked at each other. This time neither spoke but both slowly shook their heads.

"Well, what about the drummer?" Serollyn lowered her voice still more. "Was he with you the whole time you've been in the woods?"

After looking at each other again, they both nodded.

She wasn't getting anywhere. The boys were more cooperative and conversed more easily, but they seemed to have no memory of a life before coming into the forest.

"Why can't we see Tolammy?" Dedryc asked, pointing to Nestryn, who was leaning against a tree with Tolammy in her lap. "We saw him before."

"He's a life-guide, and most people can't see them," Serollyn explained. "I don't know how you saw him before, but I'd guess it had to do with the drummer." Then she had to answer questions about what a life-guide was and why she and Nestryn each had one but Marleon did not.

"But we can see Krannel," Feryn said. "Why can we see him but not Tolammy?"

Serollyn didn't understand that herself. She could only reply that life-guides were usually visible only to the one to whom they were sent. She didn't know why Krannel was an exception—a life-guide everyone could see.

"We could see the drummer, but you couldn't. And while he was drumming we could see the monkey. Why could we only see him when the drums were playing? And what about the drummer?" Dedryc wondered. "That girl called him a life-guide. She saw him, but you didn't."

"Vali only thought he was a life-guide," Serollyn said. "I don't know why he showed himself to her, but our life-guides told us he was a Sneak—a creature sent by the Death Stealers, enemies of the Life Lenders who send us our life-guides."

"And the Sneak did almost kill Tolammy," Nestryn chimed in. "If he had truly been a life-guide, he wouldn't have done that—couldn't have. Vali should realize that. I wonder if she'll ever figure it out."

"Let's hope she does, before it's too late," Serollyn said.

In the distance a great-cat howled.

"Odd," Nestryn said. "Great-cats generally don't hunt by day. You only hear them at night."

"I'm afraid of the big cats," Feryn said.

"Krannel will keep us safe," Serollyn assured him with more confidence than she felt. If Tolammy could be so grievously injured, so, she feared, could Krannel.

"He's barking. I hear him," Dedryc said, jumping up in excitement.

"You couldn't—" Serollyn began but stopped when she, too, heard the barking. It came from far off, but even so, she was amazed that Dedryc had heard him first.

She walked a short distance in the direction of the sound, straining to hear. One more short bark reached her ears, then an ominous silence.

She wanted to run to find Krannel and Marleon, but that would leave the boys and Nestryn alone. She could take the boys with her, but Nestryn, tending Tolammy, would not want to follow.

Serollyn returned to Nestryn's side. Looking at the small monkey, she asked, "Does he seem any better?"

"His breathing is steadier," Nestryn said. "He sleeps most of the time, though. I wish he'd wake up again."

Serollyn wished the same. Nestryn's life-guide was a wise counselor, and his wisdom was needed.

But Tolammy slept on, and Serollyn could only wait.

The wait was not long, though it seemed so. Krannel loped into sight, dragging by the neck a young springer, its horns mere nubs. Serollyn jumped up and ran to him, and he dropped his burden at her feet.

*Marleon comes*, he announced.

A few moments later Marleon staggered into the clearing, carrying Vali in his arms. She was unconscious, one shoulder badly mauled and bleeding heavily.

Marleon laid her down beside Nestryn. "Right after we caught the springer, we heard her scream," he explained. "We ran and found her. A great-cat had her down and had already taken a chunk out of her shoulder. The cat looked at us and slunk away like it was scared of us. I guess it didn't want to tangle with Krannel."

*I had little to do with it*, Krannel sent. *But if you wish to save your friend, you must act quickly.*

Nestryn placed Tolammy carefully on a bed of leaves and rose to her feet. "I'll look for the healing leaves," she said. "Serollyn, do what you can to stop the bleeding."

Serollyn hurried to Vali's side. Krannel left his kill and came to crouch beside her.

Marleon sank onto the ground. "I'll help you or Nestryn after I catch my breath," he said. "I had to carry her so far. Glad I found her, though."

"I wonder what happened to the Sneak," Serollyn said. "She was carrying its body."

"Don't know, since I never could see it. But she can't have it with her now."

Serollyn worked to stanch the bleeding from Vali's shoulder. As best she could, she pushed the edges of the wound together and applied pressure to slow the bleeding. It helped a little but not enough.

Marleon rose slowly. "Have to cauterize the wound," he said. "We'll lose her if we don't."

He wandered around gathering fallen branches, twigs, leaves, pieces of bark: whatever he could find that was reasonably dry. Serollyn kept pressure on Vali's wound as he set about selecting a site for the fire, laying down the larger logs, and arranging on top of them the twigs and leaves. Finally he used his flint to strike sparks off his knife blade, igniting the leaves and letting the fire spread to the twigs. He took a branch that was fresh and still had green leaves attached, stuck the leafy end in the fire, and held it there until the leaves burned off and the branch was smoldering but not flaming.

"She's still unconscious, right?" he asked.

Serollyn nodded.

"Hold her anyway. This will hurt, and it might wake her."

When Serollyn had straddled Vali, pressed her good shoulder to the ground, and held down the arm on the other side, Marleon pressed the smoldering tip of his branch to the shoulder wound. The blood sizzled and foul-smelling smoke rose from the branch. Vali jerked and screamed, then lapsed back into unconsciousness.

Marleon took the branch away and jabbed the burnt end into the ground. Serollyn examined Vali's wound. It looked ugly, but a crust had formed and the bleeding had slowed to a trickle.

"I hope she appreciates all you've done to save her," Serollyn said.

Marleon poked at the fire. "We'll need more wood to keep this going so we can roast the springer," he said. "And I'd better get the little fellow skinned and gutted."

Marleon carried the springer a distance from their camp and went to work on it. Dedryc followed and watched closely, while Feryn stood by Serollyn and gazed at Vali. The boys had been so quiet since Marleon had brought Vali that Serollyn had almost forgotten their presence.

"Feryn, please bring me my pack," Serollyn requested. "It's over there by that tree."

He fetched it and squatted beside her. "She gonna die?" he asked.

"We're doing all we can to save her," Serollyn said.

"Would she do that for you?"

"Doesn't matter." Serollyn didn't want to think about the question, much less answer it. To divert him from that topic she asked, "You and Dedryc, are you brothers?"

"Guess so," Feryn said, with a shrug of his shoulders.

"You aren't sure? Have you been together as long as you can remember?"

He nodded. "We're the woods boys," he said.

Hurriedly, to prevent his dwelling on that designation apparently given them by the Sneak, she asked, "Are you certain there's nothing at all you remember from before you came into the woods?"

He shook his head vehemently and reached a grubby finger toward Vali's wound. Serollyn swatted his hand away. "Don't touch her," she said. "Your hands are dirty."

"Why'd he bring her back?" He nodded his head in the general direction of Marleon.

Krannel growled.

"She's our friend," Serollyn said with growing impatience. "She was lost and hurt. It was the right thing to do."

He cocked his head, seeming to consider what was apparently a foreign concept to him.

"Oww!" The shout came from Dedryc.

Marleon had risen and stood over Dedryc, shaking his fist. A smear of blood on the boy's lips made Serollyn think that Marleon had struck him until she heard what Marleon was saying.

"We don't eat raw meat. And we don't eat blood—or drink it. This animal has given its life for us. It deserves our respect. We pour out its blood onto the ground as an offering of thanks to the Life Lenders. And we have not yet given praise to the animal—to this springer—for the gift of its flesh."

Serollyn left Vali to go to Dedryc. "What has he done?" she asked Marleon.

"He drank of the springer's blood," Marleon said, calmer now.

"He didn't know. He doesn't know our ways, Marleon. And he and Feryn were long in thrall to the Death Stealers. We'll teach them and they *will* learn. Be patient."

To Dedryc she said, "Life is precious and we do not take it except to preserve our own lives. The Life Lenders permit us to kill animals to meet our needs for food, but we do not profane their gift by eating without giving thanks to the slain animal and to the Life Lenders. You must learn these things."

Dedryc listened but looked puzzled. It was clear that he knew nothing of the Life Lenders and nothing of the ritual. She was convinced that wherever he and Feryn had come from, it could not have been from the clans.

"You'll learn," she told him, patting his arm. "Now come back with me, and let Marleon finish preparing the springer for roasting. When it's ready, you'll observe the rite of thanks with us. That will help you understand."

She returned to Vali, taking Dedryc with her.

"Didn't mean to make him mad," Dedryc muttered too low for Marleon to hear. "Didn't know."

"We know that," Serollyn said. "Marleon isn't mad anymore. He just got upset because, well, what you did is something our people never do."

"Won't do it again," he said too sullenly for Serollyn's liking. She bit back a sharp rebuke when Krannel's tail thumped the ground.

*They aren't that young, but they're like little children,* she sent to her life-guide.

*And because they are like small children, you must be patient with them,* he sent back.

*I try, but with so many bad things happening—*

Krannel's growl cut off her complaint. She got her canteen and her only clean wraparound from her pack, bent over Vali, wet a corner of the wraparound, and patted Vali's face with it. Vali stirred but did not waken. The bleeding from her shoulder had stopped.

*Nestryn! Where's Nestryn?* The sending came from Tolammy. Serollyn left Vali and hurried to him.

*Nestryn is gathering healing leaves for Vali,* she explained. *She'll be back soon.*

Marleon paused in his work with the springer. "Shouldn't she be back by now?

It was difficult to keep track of time here where leaves hid the sun. But, yes, Nestryn should be back.

*I must go and find her,* Tolammy sent, trying to rise.

"No," Marleon said. "You were badly hurt. I'll go."

*Finish what you're doing,* Krannel sent. *I'll go. I have a better chance of finding her than you do.*

Without giving time for an argument, Krannel bounded off and was swallowed up into the dense forest growth. In only a few minutes they heard furious barking. Marleon ran in the direction of the sound.

*I should have gone with him,* Tolammy fretted.

Serollyn was worried too, but did what she could to console Tolammy while continuing to care for Vali. A loud bang was followed by an ominous silence; Krannel's barking ceased. Serollyn ran to the edge of the clearing and peered vainly through the trees. The ever-present mist and the hanging vines obscured her view.

Dedryc came up beside her. "Sounded like a gunshot," he said.

"What do you mean? What's that?"

He shrugged.

She wanted to go after Marleon and Krannel, but she hesitated to leave Tolammy and Vali in the dubious care of Dedryc and Feryn. As she debated what to do, Nestryn hurried into the clearing carrying a bundle of leaves.

"I had to go a considerable distance to find these," she said. "And when I did find them, I found something else. The end of the forest. It's only a short walk from here.

We'll soon know what's on the far side."

*And there you must be prepared for anything.*

"Oh, Tolammy, you're awake!" She thrust the leaves into Serollyn's hands and ran to her life-guide, picked him up, and hugged him.

"Nestryn, you'll have to take care of Vali," Serollyn said. "I'm going to look for Marleon and Krannel."

"What—?"

There was no time to explain. Serollyn handed the leaves to Feryn and headed off in the direction she thought the sounds had come from. She had gone only a short distance when she heard brush crackling behind her and turned to see Dedryc limping after her.

"Stay with Feryn," she ordered.

He ignored the order and caught up with her. "Be careful," he warned.

"Of course I'll be careful," she said crossly. "You go back."

But he tugged on her arm and held her back. At that moment Marleon and Krannel burst through the undergrowth. Her relief was so great that she hugged Marleon first and then threw her arms around Krannel.

Marleon looked bemused at her greeting, but Krannel squirmed free of her embrace. *We need to go back to the others,* he sent.

"What's wrong?"

"Hunters," Marleon said. "Not our people. They have metal tubes that shoot fire."

"Guns," Dedryc said. "Those are guns."

"Whatever they are," Marleon went on, "they shot fire at us. They missed me and just singed Krannel's ear. But they're coming this way."

Serollyn saw blood dripping from the missing tip of Krannel's ear. *Never mind that,* he sent in response to her alarmed exclamation. *Do as Marleon says.*

So they hurried back to where the others waited, and there Krannel allowed her to press to his ear some of the healing leaves Nestryn had brought for Vali. She was still fussing over him when two men stepped into the clearing. They wore clothes different from any Serollyn had seen. She guessed that the two garments each wore must be the "shirt" and "trousers" described by tribal hunters who had encountered men from the far side of the forest and spoken with them. A leaf-green garment covered the top of their bodies from neck to below the waist, hiding even the flesh of their arms as far as the wrists. A deep brown garment covered them from the waist down, dividing into two parts to enclose each leg separately, its ends tucked into in high boots that rose to cover the lower portion of their legs.

Dedryc gave a cry of fear and Feryn ran to huddle next to Nestryn, who was caring for Vali. Serollyn straightened and remained beside Krannel.

The men fastened their gazes on Marleon. "Boy, you scared away our prey," one said.

"You were trying to kill Krannel," Marleon responded, pointing at Serollyn's life-guide.

"That dog? Don't be stupid. We didn't come into the woods to hunt a dog. I'm talking about the great-cat we had in our sights. Would've got it if you hadn't spooked it."

"I didn't see any great-cat," Marleon said.

"Why would you try to kill a great-cat?" Serollyn asked. "I wouldn't think they'd be good eating."

"Eating?" The second man laughed. "No, I wouldn't want to eat one."

"Then why would you kill it?" Nestryn asked.

"Why not?" the man countered. "They're dangerous animals, and the head and pelt make a good trophy."

"You'd kill a magnificent animal like a great-cat to display its head and pelt?"

Marleon's incredulous reaction brought more laughter from the men. "What else?" one asked. "And what're kids like you doing out here in the woods?"

"We're passing through them," Serollyn said, snapping off the words in anger.

"Looks like you've been doing some hunting, too." The hunter indicated the springer Marleon had been preparing.

"We hunt for food only," Marleon said. "We'll cook this meat as soon as I've finished preparing it. If you're hungry, we'll be glad to share."

It was the proper thing to say, but Serollyn hoped the men would turn down the invitation. These men weren't of their people. She didn't want them around.

"Well, isn't that good of you," one of the two said, walking over and peering down at the springer. "Funny way to butcher it. Looks like you spilled all its blood."

"Of course I did," Marleon said. "We don't eat the blood. And we give thanks to the animal for giving its life for us."

"And to the Life Lenders for providing it," Serollyn chimed in.

The men laughed again. They seemed to find the whole situation amusing. Serollyn liked them less by the minute.

"Where are you children from?" one man asked.

"We aren't children," Nestryn put in indignantly. "And what business is it of yours where we're from?"

"Don't get smart with us, little girl," the man said with a sneer.

The other man pointed his weapon in her direction. Serollyn cast a nervous glance at Krannel's wounded ear and hoped Nestryn would be more cautious. Like Dedryc and Feryn, these men had no life-guides.

"We don't mean you harm," the man said, his aimed weapon belying his words. "We just want to know why you're here and where you're from. By the funny way you're dressed we know you aren't local."

"Why do you care?" Marleon asked. "Do you own this forest?"

"We own hunting rights in it," the man answered, scowling at Marleon. "Exclusive rights to hunt in this particular section. So you have no business here."

Serollyn judged by their angry expressions that Marleon and Nestryn were disposed to argue. She spoke hurriedly. "We didn't know we were trespassing. We've never heard of exclusive hunting rights. We hunt only what we need for food, and we're only passing through. I believe we're near the edge of the woods now. We wish only to reach it and leave the forest."

"Well, since you're just kids and you invited us to share the meat you caught, we'll overlook your trespassing this time. Where are you heading?"

"We're taking these boys home," Serollyn said, indicating Dedryc and Feryn, who were still cowering near Nestryn and Marleon.

"Where do they live? And what're they so scared of?

We said we weren't going to punish you."

"They're easily frightened. We found them here in the forest," Serollyn said, wanting to give as little information as possible. "We want to find their home and return them to their parents."

One of the men walked near Feryn, who immediately darted behind Marleon.

"I'm not planning to hurt you, boy," the man said, showing his teeth in a smile that held no friendliness.

"Stay away from him," Marleon said.

"Bet they're twins," the man said. "There's lots of folks so superstitious about twins that they take 'em into the forest to die."

"But that's terrible!" Serollyn exclaimed.

The other hunter approached from an angle that allowed him to see Vali lying behind Nestryn and Krannel. "Looks like somebody got hurt," the man said. "That's what happens when kids like you go exploring where you've got no business going. Better let us have a look at her."

"We're taking care of her," Nestryn said, placing herself between Vali and the hunter. "She'll recover."

"Looks bad off to me," the hunter said, bending down for a closer look.

Krannel growled. The man kicked at him but missed. "Call off your dog," he said.

"He won't hurt you," Serollyn said, trying to keep the peace. "He just doesn't want you to go near Vali."

"That the girl's name? Guess we should introduce ourselves. I'm Landgrave Wilder and my partner's Landgrave Munck. Now who're you and, again, where are you from?"

Landgrave must be some sort of title, but it was not one that Serollyn recognized. She introduced her friends. "I'm Serollyn, he's Marleon, and she's Nestryn." Serollyn pointed to each as she named them. "And that's Krannel." She pointed to her life-guide but decided not to say that he was far more than a dog.

"Okay, but you haven't answered my other question. Where are you from?" The emphasis he put on the repeated question held menace.

"We told you we came through the forest," Serollyn said.

"Don't tell him anything else," Marleon snapped.

"Why so secretive? What you running away from?" Wilder persisted, while Munck held his weapon in a threatening pose.

"We aren't running away from anything," Nestryn said.

"Oh, yeah? Kids like you out in the woods by yourselves, nothing but a dog to protect you? No question you're runaways, and I wouldn't be surprised if your folks weren't worried enough about you to pay a reward to anybody that brought you back."

"Nobody is looking for us, and nobody would pay you anything," Marleon said a bit too quickly.

"You know something?" Munck asked, placing his face so close to Marleon's that their noses nearly touched. "I don't believe you."

"Neither do I," Wilder said. "You couldn't have come all the way through this forest. And the way those boys there are acting," he indicated Dedryc and Feryn, "I'd say you—or at least those two—are guilty of something bad."

"No one is guilty of anything," Marleon snapped.

*Stay calm and be courteous,* Tolammy sent. *If these men threaten you with harm, I will act to protect you.*

*Please be careful,* Nestryn sent. *You're not fully recovered, and I don't want you hurt again.*

Serollyn understood her friend's concern. But Tolammy couldn't be seen, so he was safer than the rest of them. Anything Krannel tried to do could get him killed. These men not only didn't regard him as a life-guide; they seemed to have no idea of what a life-guide was.

Just as Dedryc and Feryn didn't. If their lack of understanding about life-guides and the Life Lenders was typical of the people on this far side of the forest, Serollyn no longer wanted to go there.

Finished preparing the springer, Marleon rigged a spit, placed the cleaned carcass on it, and set it over their fire, which he built up, adding leaves and branches from the forest floor.

"Good at that, aren't you, kid?" Munck said. "Where'd you learn it?"

"I was trained by my father and older brothers," Marleon said, heeding Krannel's advice, though Serollyn could tell by his tone that he found it hard to be courteous to these boorish men.

The savory odor of roasting meat soon permeated the clearing. Wilder and Munck settled themselves on a wide root. Although they hadn't said they accepted the invitation to share the meal, apparently they intended to stay. Munck held his gun across his knees and fondled the stock lovingly from time to time. "Pretty, isn't it?" he asked, seeing Serollyn watching him. He pointed to the shiny metal carved into intricate shapes and set into the wooden stock. "Pretty and deadly."

With a shudder Serollyn turned away. How could anything deadly be pretty?

Wilder took off the goatskin bag he carried over his shoulder, took tools from it, and worked on his gun. He grinned and said, "Have to clean and reload this rifle so it's ready to fire again. But don't worry. Landgrave Munck hasn't fired his. See, he's got it half-cocked and ready."

Serollyn didn't understand the terms he used, but she understood the meaning: Munck could fire his gun, or rifle as he'd called it, at any time.

*Krannel,* she sent, *how can we get rid of these men?*

*Be patient,* Krannel urged. *Do not antagonize them. Tolammy and I are trying to work out a plan.*

So communication was passing between the life-guides that she was not privy to—and neither, she assumed, was Nestryn.

A groan alerted her that Vali was waking—and at the worst possible time. Vali, who could hear neither life-guide and could not see Tolammy, would not be disposed to cooperate. Serollyn cast a desperate look at Nestryn.

But Nestryn could only shrug and look worried along with Serollyn.

"Seems like your friend's coming to," Wilder observed.

Vali's eyelids fluttered then opened. She sat up. With Tolammy perched on her shoulder, Nestryn moved quickly to Vali's side. Marleon left off tending the roasting springer and stood alert. Krannel rose from where he'd been lying and stood at Serollyn's side.

Vali sat up and looked around wild-eyed. Her gaze fastened on Marleon. She raised her good arm and pointed at him. "You. You did this," she said. "You sent your great-cat to attack me."

# 13

# MAGISTRATE

"Vali, Marleon and Krannel saved you from the great-cat," Nestryn said in a soothing voice.

"Isn't Marleon's life-guide a great-cat? He sent it to attack me because I was running away."

"But Vali," Nestryn tried to reason with her, "you saw the great-cat that attacked you, didn't you? If it had been a life-guide, you wouldn't have seen it."

"Why not? I see Krannel. Everyone does."

Wilder looked up from his work on his gun. "Ha! I knew you kids were running away from something."

"But what's this life-guide stuff?" Munck asked, his brow furrowed in bewilderment.

"Some game they're playing," Wilder said. "Or some superstition. Doesn't matter. This girl says they sent a great-cat to maul her, and she's been mauled, sure enough."

Munck scratched his head. "Don't see how they could control a great-cat," he said.

"We can't," Serollyn put in quickly. "Marleon saved her life. We've told you that."

"They killed my life-guide," Vali wailed, trying to rise.

"They tried to kill me."

"Vali, you know that isn't true," Nestryn said, restraining her.

"Seems like we might've found out why you kids are on the run," Wilder said.

"You'd believe her over all the rest of us?" Marleon demanded angrily.

"She's hurt, no denying that," Munck said.

"We didn't hurt her."

"Maybe, maybe not," Wilder said. "After we eat your roast, we'll get you back to town and let the magistrate figure this out."

Alarmed, Serollyn sent, *Krannel, what do we do? Is it safe to go with them?*

*Little is safe for you now. But I think you must go,* her life-guide sent, moving to stand close beside her. *Vali's claims have made it too dangerous for Tolammy and me to carry out our plan. The alternative is to fight, but against their weapons you would have little chance. And make no mistake: they would not hesitate to use those weapons.*

Serollyn knew that Nestryn heard Krannel's sending, and by his frown and the firm set of his jaw she could tell that Marleon had heard, too, and didn't like the idea.

Marleon tended the roasting springer while Nestryn prepared fern sprouts and mushrooms she gathered beneath nearby trees. The meal, when it was served, was the best they'd had in days, but only the two hunters seemed to enjoy it. Dedryc and Feryn ate little; Vali refused to eat at all. Marleon picked at his food; Nestryn ate because, she said, she knew it was important to keep up her strength. And Serollyn gave most of her share to Krannel.

After they ate, Wilder and Munck barely gave them time to gather their things and break camp. The two hunters herded them along at a pace too rapid for Vali, who was still quite weak and complained loudly of the pain in her injured shoulder. The hunters ordered Marleon and Serollyn to rig a makeshift litter and carry her between them. They tried to force Dedryc and Feryn to help, but the boys only crowded against Nestryn and shook their heads vehemently. They had scarcely spoken since the hunters arrived, and their fear was almost palpable.

As they progressed, the forest thinned and the light increased despite the lateness of the day. Nestryn and Serollyn changed places; Nestryn took up one end of the litter while Serollyn did her best to comfort Dedryc and Feryn.

They emerged from the woods into a field of tall grass and weeds tipped with burs that clung to their clothing and scratched their legs. They had to hold the litter high to pass through the weeds, but soon they reached cultivated fields, where they walked between crops growing in neat rows.

Serollyn saw buildings in the distance and guessed that they were homes, though they looked very different from the sort of homes she was familiar with, being larger, with roofs covered with thick slates rather than the thatch used by her people. She hoped that they were the hunters' destination; she was weary, and her arms and shoulders ached from carrying the litter.

But the hunters drove them past the houses, toward a high wall over which she could see larger buildings, many of stone. They reached a gate in the wall, and through this the hunters guided their exhausted captives—how Serollyn thought of herself and her friends. She could hardly think otherwise. The hunters' weapons had remained aimed at them throughout their long trek.

Tired as she was, Serollyn knew that Marleon must be even more so. She and Nestryn had switched off from bearing the litter several more times, but Marleon had had no relief from carrying his end. He had never complained, though his weariness etched hard lines in his face.

Night had fallen by the time they passed through the gates, but bright light streamed from the buildings and flames in glass bulbs on high poles lit the streets.

Few people were in the streets, but those they did see, men and women and a few children, all stopped and stared at their procession until Wilder and Munck warned them on their way. Serollyn saw no life-guides; none of the people had them.

These streets gave Serollyn a closed-in feeling, as though the weight of the buildings on either side was pressing down on her. She tried to tell herself her tiredness and the unfamiliarity of the place caused these feelings.

She thought that she must be hallucinating when as they passed one of the poles that held the lights, she thought she saw, partly blended with Marleon's shadow, a shadow shaped like a great-cat.

"Turn right at the next corner," Wilder called out.

Serollyn coaxed Dedryc and Feryn forward. The boys were nearly asleep on their feet. Marleon and Nestryn carried the litter around the indicated corner, and the others plodded after them. They went only a few paces before coming to wide stone steps leading to the largest building Serollyn had yet seen. Its imposing façade, with its stone carvings and wide, brightly lit windows, loomed like some monster out of the darkest myths.

Wilder directed them to ascend the stairs, and when they had done so, he banged on doors of embossed metal.

The doors swung open with a suddenness that nearly unbalanced Marleon, who had to bend backward to avoid being struck by them. Wilder motioned them through the open doors. When Krannel would have entered with them, the man who had opened the doors said, "You can't bring that dog in here. You'll have to chain him outside."

It would do no good to protest that Krannel was a life-guide. Serollyn suspected that these people had no knowledge of life-guides. "He doesn't need to be chained," she said. "He'll wait for us on the steps."

"He vicious?" the man asked, looking closely at Krannel.

Serollyn assured him that Krannel was not, and the man grudgingly assented to let Krannel remain on the steps unbound. "You'll have nobody but yourself to blame if he runs off," he warned.

"He won't run off," Serollyn snapped.

"Know a man had a dog looked like him," the man persisted maddeningly. "He ran off into the forest, and his owner never found him."

"Well, if you think he'll run off, let him come inside with me," Serollyn said, too tired to want more than to go where she could rest.

"Can't do that. Unless you let me chain him, we'll just have to hope you're right about him."

*Don't worry about me,* Krannel sent. *I won't leave. If you need me, call. I'll find a way to get inside.*

The man turned and led them into a long hall. "Wait here," he instructed and strode the length of the hall to pass through a door at its end.

"You can put that litter down now," Landgrave Munck said, still keeping his weapon trained on them.

Marleon and Nestryn lowered their burden to the floor. With a sigh, Marleon rubbed his arms and shoulders.

They waited for some time before the man who had let them in returned and announced in a loud voice, "Magistrate Pell." The portly older man who entered wore a long red robe with gold trim around its collar and the cuffs of its long sleeves. Serollyn had never seen such a silly outfit.

Wilder and Munck both bowed, and Wilder said, "Magistrate, we went hunting and found these children wandering in our preserve. They claimed to have been unaware that they were trespassing, and that I believe, but this girl who is badly injured has made serious charges against them that we felt you should hear."

Vali, who had been either asleep or unconscious during the latter part of the trek, now awoke and tried to sit up. Nestryn bent to help her, but Vali pushed her away.

"They tried to kill me," she declared.

"Bring them into the courtroom," the robed man said. He turned to lead the way.

Marleon was forced to take up the litter once more. Serollyn took the other end. They were led to a large room with several benches and a raised platform with a high table, a high-backed wooden chair behind it. The magistrate stepped onto this platform and sat in the chair. The man who'd opened the door for them bustled about, placing a pitcher of water and a glass on the magistrate's table, along with a small wooden hammer.

"That will do, Stalwart Crinston," the magistrate said. "This is only a brief, informal hearing."

The man he'd called Stalwart Crinston bowed and retreated to the rear of the room.

Marleon and Serollyn lowered the litter, and Vali again sat up. This time Wilder assisted her, and she did not push him away as she had Nestryn. He helped her stand briefly and sit on the bench directly in front of the high table. Munck motioned the others to seats on the bench behind that one, and he sat behind them, his rifle at his side.

Vali repeated her accusations. Serollyn didn't listen; she was tired of hearing the baseless complaints. She let her mind drift, reaching that state of near-sleep where the boundaries between dream and reality blur.

She thought she saw Krannel on the steps outside the building, but something was wrong. A heavy chain wound around his neck. They'd agreed not to chain him. They'd broken their word!

She looked further. The chain—a man was holding the other end of it, a man she'd never seen before. He dragged Krannel down the steps. Krannel tried to resist, but the chain choked him. He had to go with the man.

When they reached the street, Krannel tried to pull free. The man aimed a hard kick at Krannel's ribs. His mouth opened in what must have been a yelp, though Serollyn heard no sound. The man dragged Krannel down the street.

Her eyes popped open. Serollyn jumped to her feet. "Krannel!" she burst out. "I've got to get to Krannel!"

The magistrate started, adjusted the collar of his robe, and glared at her. "Young lady, this is an informal hearing, but that does not give you the right to interrupt the proceedings with such an outburst."

"But my life-guide—my dog—he's in trouble." She was certain that what she had seen had not been a mere dream. She could not get a response to her frantic mindsendings.

"We wanted to chain him," Wilder said. "You wouldn't permit it."

"But a man put a chain on him and took him away. I saw it." Serollyn was sobbing now.

"Young lady," the magistrate said with exaggerated patience, "you cannot see through walls. You've fallen asleep and had a nightmare. I suggest you collect yourself and make a greater effort to stay awake for the rest of this hearing."

*I'll check on Krannel*, Tolammy sent.

It was his assurance rather than the magistrate's admonition that let Serollyn compose herself and settle back into her seat. Nestryn's life-guide would do his best to learn what, if anything, had happened to Krannel.

Vali was still telling her story, a mixture of erroneous assumptions, wild accusations, and outright lies, with a slight sprinkling of truth. Her convoluted tale quite clearly confused the magistrate, since it involved life-guides, wood boys, and a great-cat, which she insisted had been deliberately set on her by Marleon.

"I've never seen a great-cat in our preserve," Wilder said, shaking his head. "There aren't that many in the woods, and the few there are stay much deeper in the forest. They have plenty of game; they don't need to wander into the verges."

"There's nothing to stop one from coming," Munck put in. "But I don't understand this life-guide business, or how this boy could make a great-cat attack at his bidding."

Frustrated and probably in pain, Vali cried out, "Why don't you understand? Don't any of you have life-guides?"

"I have no idea what you mean by 'life-guides'," the magistrate declared in a disgusted tone.

"Magistrate Pell, sir, they've been ranting about them since we came on them in our woods," Munck said.

"I've heard the term before," Crinston said, coming forward from his post by the rear door. "There's a crazy woman waits tables at San's Place and talks to herself all the time, nattering on about things that make no sense. Nobody pays her much attention. But I've heard her mumble something about a life-guide often enough that the phrase stuck in my mind."

Marleon leaned forward. "What's this woman's name?" he asked.

Crinston shrugged. "I never asked. I think I've heard them call her Jaxie or Joxie or something like that."

*Joxie.* Serollyn's heart leaped. Her mother's name was Joxlyn. Could it be …?

She had to know! She had to get out of this place, first find Krannel, and then search out the place called San's. She must learn whether the woman waiting tables there was her mother.

But Munck still sat behind her with his rifle. And Tolammy had not returned.

# 14

# GREAT-CAT

Serollyn paid no attention to the proceedings. She thought about the woman they'd called "crazy," a woman who might be her mother. She couldn't understand why neither Tolammy nor Krannel had mindsent, and she was frantic with worry about Krannel.

When Vali let out a loud wail, Serollyn had no idea why. Marleon saw her confusion and explained. "The magistrate couldn't make sense of Vali's story and said he didn't think we meant to go into the private part of the forest, so he's not charging you with anything."

Magistrate Pell rose, gathered his robe about him, and stepped down from the platform. He came to stand directly in front of the benches where they all sat.

"I don't know where you young people come from, but it's clear you don't know our customs. I can't just turn you loose to wander around town at night. I'll have Stalwart Crinston take you to a safe place."

"I won't go with them," Vali said. "They did try to kill me, even if you don't believe me. Anyway, I can't walk."

Serollyn was sure Vali could walk if she wanted to, but she said nothing. Vali would only slow them down, and Serollyn had to find Krannel.

The magistrate regarded Vali thoughtfully. "I suppose," he said, "you could remain here in the care of my housekeeper. She can put you into a guest room. In the morning I'll have a doctor in to see about your wound."

"Yes, please," Vali said eagerly, while Serollyn wondered what a "housekeeper" was. Possibly it was these peoples' word for "wife."

"We should all stay together," Marleon objected.

"I don't have room for all of you," the magistrate said. "Stalwart Crinston will take the rest of you to a suitable lodging. I'll fetch my housekeeper to see to your friend."

Fearing that Marleon would offer further objection, Serollyn said, "I have to see about Krannel."

*And I have to see where Tolammy is,* Nestryn sent, looking just as worried as Serollyn felt.

But at that moment Tolammy scampered in and leaped onto Nestryn's shoulder.

"I'm sure your dog will be where you left him—unless he's wandered off," Crinston said, his tone patronizing. "You said he wouldn't do that."

*I couldn't find him,* Tolammy said, hanging his head. His tail drooped. *I followed his scent for some distance, to a large brick building. I've been so long because I hoped to find a way to get inside, but the windows were boarded and the door was tightly locked. I climbed up to the roof hoping to find a vent or some type of opening, but there was nothing. I tried to mindspeak but got no response, so I was forced to return with no news. All I can do is lead you to the building.*

*He's not dead, is he?* Serollyn sent desperately, brushing past Crinston to get closer to Tolammy.

*If he were dead, I'd know it, and so would you,* the monkey reassured her, but then added, confirming her own

119

suspicion, *I fear he is unconscious, since I know no other reason why he wouldn't have responded to me or spoken to you.*

During this exchange Crinston had herded them all from the room and back to the building's entrance. Nestryn quickly filled Tolammy in on what had happened with the magistrate.

Munck and Wilder walked behind them, whispering. Serollyn couldn't hear what they were saying, but she knew they were angry about the magistrate's decision. They might take matters into their own hands once they were clear of the building. And she was not inclined to trust Crinston, either.

Outside, the steps where Krannel had been left were empty, as Serollyn had known they would be.

"Guess your dog wandered off, after all," Crinston commented with a grin that Serollyn didn't like at all.

*I'm sure that man had something to do with Krannel's disappearance,* she sent. *We have to get away.*

Marleon nodded.

*It won't be easy while they're carrying those gun things,* Nestryn sent.

*Don't try anything now,* Tolammy cautioned. *They're taking us in the direction we need to go to reach the building I told you about.*

They continued walking over rounded stones that paved the street. The stones did not make for comfortable walking, and Serollyn stumbled several times, Marleon grabbing her arm and steadying her each time. Finally he kept hold of her arm, at first cupping his palm around her elbow, then sliding his hand down until his fingers intertwined with hers.

They walked only a little farther along the street when

Tolammy sent, *Here is where we need to turn.*

It was at a place where another street crossed theirs. Serollyn thought for a moment that the men might be heading for the place where Krannel was a captive, but they continued straight on.

*We have to get away from them,* Serollyn sent, and stumbled, falling against Marleon and bringing them both to a halt.

"What's wrong, girl?" Wilder asked, while Crinston, in the lead, looked back to see why they had stopped.

"Nothing," Serollyn said. "I—I just stumbled and twisted my ankle a bit."

"You can walk, can't you?" Munck asked with not the slightest hint of sympathy.

She nodded, and Crinston beckoned and headed forward.

*We've got to get to Krannel.* She feigned a bad limp.

Dedryc and Feryn had been walking quietly beside Nestryn and behind Serollyn and Marleon, but now Dedryc spoke. "We need to go that way," he said, tugging at Serollyn's hand and pointing up the intersecting street.

"Why do you say that?" Serollyn asked. He couldn't have received any of the exchange with Tolammy. She continued to hold back.

"Kid doesn't know anything," Munck said. "Just wants to make trouble."

Crinston stopped and looked back with impatience. "I'm taking you where Magistrate Pell wants you to go," he said. "You can't go haring off anywhere you please."

*I'd guess, based on his earlier connection with the Death Stealers' Sneak, that the boy does know something,* Tolammy sent. *He may sense the presence of a Sneak, and that may mean that the Sneak has Krannel. We must get away from these men.*

*How can we get away, when they have those long gun things?* Nestryn sent back. *I'm very afraid they're leading us into some sort of trap.*

"I'm scared," Feryn said in a small voice. He was clinging to Nestryn.

The behavior of Dedryc and Feryn convinced Serollyn Tolammy was right about the involvement of the Sneak. *We need to act right now to save Krannel,* she sent.

Nestryn sent her agreement, and Marleon nodded. He released Serollyn's arm and stepped behind her, putting himself between her and Wilder and Munck with their guns. "Run!" he shouted, pushing her. Dedryc sped off on his own in the direction Tolammy had indicated.

She ran after him, and heard Nestryn follow. She didn't look back to see whether Feryn had come along.

A loud blast brought her to a halt. She spun around.

Marleon was grappling with Munck. Wilder, his gun smoking, was swinging the weapon like a club, aiming for Marleon's head. Serollyn let out a scream. Feryn stopped but Nestryn kept running, Tolammy on her shoulder. "I'm going after Dedryc," she called.

Serollyn knew she should join Nestryn, but her attention was focused on Marleon.

There was another blast, from Munck's gun, and the noise and jerk of the gun drove Marleon back. The barrel of Wilder's gun connected with Marleon's head, toppling him to the street. Serollyn started back toward him.

From out of nowhere a dark shape leaped onto Wilder. A shadow acquiring substance, the thing roared and tore at Wilder. A great-cat!

Munck frantically stuffed powder into a funnel-like

contraption attached to his gun. The cat's attack had made Wilder drop his gun. Serollyn ran for it, grabbed it up, and in imitation of what Wilder had done, swung it like a club at Munck.

Her aim wasn't as good as Wilder's had been. She missed Munck but hit the gun he was loading and knocked it from his hands. With a snarl Munck grabbed the gun Serollyn held and yanked it from her.

And toppled beside her, tackled by Feryn, who jerked his legs out from under him.

The great-cat finished with Wilder and leaped onto Munck. Feryn backed away and huddled near the street. Serollyn sat up and scooted to Marleon's side. He groaned and opened his eyes; she helped him sit up.

The great-cat's growls drew his attention. He stared transfixed as the cat left bleeding claw marks down Munck's face and neck, then sat back on its haunches and regarded its prey.

Serollyn could see it clearly in the light cast by the streetlamp—a beautiful animal, large and sleek. It turned its head, and the light reflected in its eyes turned them silver. It fixed its gaze on Marleon.

Marleon struggled to his feet and returned the creature's gaze. The animal neither moved nor blinked.

Marleon walked forward, coming to a halt in front of it. He threw his arms around the great-cat's neck. "Radic!"

## 15

## VICTOR AND VANQUISHED

Serollyn stared in amazement as the great-cat licked blood from Marleon's face. "Are you sure—"

"Of course I'm sure," Marleon broke in. He gave the cat another hug.

"I haven't heard him say anything," Serollyn said. "Has he mindsent?"

"Not yet. But you will, won't you?" He ruffled the cat's fur.

The doubt that nagged at Serollyn grew greater when Feryn jumped up, ran to her, and clung, trembling.

"Do you see the great-cat?" she asked.

He nodded, apparently too frightened to speak.

"Why shouldn't he see Radic?" Marleon asked with a sharpness Serollyn didn't like. "He sees Krannel."

"Everyone sees Krannel," she said.

"So why shouldn't Radic be like Krannel?"

Serollyn didn't have an answer. Nestryn and Tolammy had disappeared into the distance. They couldn't waste time arguing. "We have to hurry," she said. "Without Tolammy we won't know where to go."

Marleon nodded and straightened. Radic, if it was truly he, loped ahead of them. Serollyn gave a single glance behind her to be certain they were in no danger from Munck and Wilder. The men lay where they had fallen. Crinston was nowhere in sight.

She ran after Marleon and caught up with him. The blow he'd taken from Wilder was slowing his steps. She was worried about him, but the urgency of following Nestryn and Dedryc and finding Krannel kept her from expressing her concern. She saved her breath for running.

She caught Marleon's hand and held it as she ran, pulling him along with her. Feryn trailed behind them, drawing even with them only when the great-cat raced ahead. Maybe it was following the trail that she and Marleon could not sense.

As she ran, in rhythm with her pounding feet, she mindsent, *Krannel, Krannel, Krannel.* The desperately desired response failed to come.

She did pick up a brief sending from Tolammy: *Beware! Danger!* It might have been directed to her and Marleon, or to Nestryn, or even to Krannel. She couldn't tell. She already knew they were heading into danger. Could the message warn of danger accompanying them?

Briefly she lost sight of the great-cat, but a loud howl told her he wasn't far in front of them.

As she and Marleon continued to run, a scream rang out. Nestryn, she thought. And more howls and snarls.

Serollyn and Marleon reached an intersection, looked along the intersecting street, and saw a terrifying sight: not one but two great-cats, locked in fierce battle, with Nestryn backed against a wall, Dedryc cowering beside her and Tolammy clinging to her neck.

The two large cats fought ferociously, biting, clawing, rising up on their hind legs to attack. Already both were bleeding from numerous gouges and deep scratches.

Serollyn and Marleon drew as near as they dared. "Which one's your life-guide?" Serollyn asked.

Marleon leaned against the wall of a building for support. "I can't tell," he said, breathing hard, as much from fear as from their desperate run, Serollyn suspected.

To reach Nestryn and Dedryc they'd have to pass the brawling cats and risk he danger of being clawed or bitten. At this late hour the streets had been largely deserted, but the yowls and growls of the cats were drawing men and a few women from nearby buildings. One man had what Serollyn recognized as a gun, though it was plainer and smaller than those Wilder and Munck had wielded. She nudged Marleon and pointed.

"No!" he shouted, and leaped toward the cats.

Serollyn grabbed for him to pull him back. Too late! He burst into the midst of the fight, received a vicious swipe from the paw of one cat, and backed into the jaws of the other. Those jaws closed—but only over Marleon's wraparound. The cat lifted him aside, nearly pulling the wraparound off him but getting him safely out of the battle zone and onto the same side of the street as the man with the gun.

Marleon didn't hesitate; he ran to the man, shouting, "Don't hurt the cats. Let them fight it out."

Fortunately, the gathering crowd seemed to agree, though not for the same reason. Marleon wanted to spare his life-guide; the crowd wanted to see the fight.

"I'll wager on the one that's on top now," a man shouted.

"But look at how that one's bleeding!" A woman yelled back.

The man with the gun kept it aimed at the cats but made no move to shoot it. He said something Serollyn couldn't hear that must have eased Marleon's mind. He could now make his way to Nestryn, Dedryc, and Tolammy. Serollyn wanted desperately to know what the monkey thought about the cats, but Tolammy did not reply to her frantic sendings.

What was both clear and puzzling to Serollyn was that all of the gathered throng, none of whom seemed to have life-guides, could apparently see both great-cats. Of course, Krannel was visible to everyone, and Marleon's life-guide might be, as well. But what was the other great-cat? Not a life-guide, certainly. She suspected it might be the Sneak. Tolammy had said it would reappear in a different form, but she hadn't expected it to be visible to everyone.

And where was Feryn? Serollyn suddenly realized that he had disappeared when they encountered the warring great-cats.

The great-cats were rolling on the ground now, one's mouth at the other's throat. If only she knew which one was Radic. He must have been the one that had lifted Marleon out of the way, but the cats were in constant motion, making it impossible to tell which one that was.

The cat that had its teeth in the other's throat gave a shake; a great gout of blood poured from the torn throat, and one cat lay still. The other stood, placed a paw on the shoulder of its opponent, and let out a mighty roar.

The man with the gun aimed it at the victorious cat. The crowd had fallen silent, faces registering awe and fear. Marleon again called out, "Don't shoot!"

Dedryc lifted his head toward the sky and howled, an

inhuman sound that drew everyone's attention, including the gunman's, away from the cat.

Looking for Feryn, Serollyn edged along the side of the building, avoiding the cat still standing over its foe, until she was far enough past to cross in front of the crowd, which was keeping a prudent distance from the roaring cat. She made her way to Marleon and Nestryn.

"Is that Radic?" she asked Marleon as soon as she reached them.

"I think so," he said, keeping an eye on the man with the gun.

"What's wrong with Dedryc?" The boy had just let out a second howl.

"I don't know," Nestryn said, and burst into tears. "I can't get Tolammy to tell me anything."

Indeed, the little monkey sat with head bowed and eyes closed as though asleep. Serollyn added his health to her growing list of worries. Dedryc, though, headed that list.

She slipped her arms around Dedryc. "What's wrong?" she asked. "What is it?"

His only answer was another howl. The crowd closed in around them, Dedryc and his howls providing a new attraction, now that the battle of the great-cats had ended. Most did cast nervous glances over their shoulders at the victor of that battle. But the great-cat made no threatening moves and seemed uninterested, almost unaware, of the crowd.

Tolammy's head jerked up. His eyes popped open. He looked around as if only now aware of his surroundings.

*The great-cat,* he sent. *Is it alive or dead?*

*I think one killed the other,* Serollyn sent back.

*I know about their fight,* Tolammy returned. *But the fallen one—are you certain it's dead?*

*No,* Serollyn sent, puzzled. *But blood just poured from its throat. Is the cat that won really Marleon's life-guide?*

*I fear not,* Tolammy responded. *Dedryc howls because he senses the danger of having their link with the Sneak reestablished. Where is Feryn?*

*I don't know. He ran when he saw the cats fighting, and I lost sight of him.*

*That strengthens my suspicion that one cat is the Sneak,* returned. *If the fallen cat still lives, it must be kept alive to keep Feryn and Dedryc free.*

*I don't understand—"* Serollyn began.

*Don't try. Just see about the great-cat.*

She looked at Nestryn, who nodded. Together they pushed their way through the crowd, Tolammy riding on Nestryn's shoulder, Marleon and Dedryc following close behind.

The crowd parted to let them pass, but reformed behind them, turning to keep all eyes focused on the strange happenings. Some were muttering; some were calling out questions or demands. Serollyn heard it all as noise and ignored it.

They reached the great-cats, and looking closely at the fallen one, Serollyn saw a slight rise and fall of its side. It lived, though its eyes were glazed and its mouth lolled open. Blood seeped from the throat wound to add to the pool beneath its head and neck.

She knelt beside the dying animal. The other cat let out an ominous growl.

"How can I be certain which is Radic?" Marleon asked, his voice anguished.

Nestryn knelt beside Serollyn and reached out to touch the cat. With another snarl, the victor cat hunched, ready to pounce.

*Get back,* Tolammy warned, and Nestryn scooted back.

Tolammy leaped from her shoulder onto the ground beside the dying cat. Nestryn gasped, and Serollyn waited for the angry great-cat to leap on the monkey. Instead it remained still, its gaze fixed on Nestryn as if daring her to return to its foe.

It didn't see Tolammy. It couldn't be a life-guide. It had taken the form of Marleon's imagined life-guide as it had earlier taken the form of Vali's.

*Nestryn, you still have healing leaves in your pack,* Tolammy sent. *Give them to me.*

Nestryn shrugged out of her pack, opened it, and extracted the small wad of leaves, now badly wilted, that Serollyn had watched her stuff into it early that same day. Serollyn stepped forward, risking attack by the great-cat to stand where she blocked his view of Nestryn while Nestryn handed the leaves to Tolammy and Tolammy pressed them onto the neck wound. The leaves had eased the pain and redness of the ant bites that had afflicted Dedryc and Feryn, but would they be effective against the grievous wound suffered by the great-cat?

A low, angry rumble came from the throat of the great-cat standing at Marleon's side. Serollyn was sure that the only thing preventing it from attacking was its desire to deceive Marleon.

*Tolammy, can it hear our mindspeech?*

Tolammy was too busy to respond. Nestryn pulled her back, away from the dangerous cat at Marleon's side. Tolammy was chewing the leaves into a paste and smearing it into and over the neck wound. He worked rapidly yet methodically, until the area was covered with the paste.

*Do you think that can possibly help?* Serollyn sent to Nestryn.

*Tolammy thinks so,* her friend sent back.

Marleon looked from one to the other. He must have received the sending and had questions, but, unable to mindsend, he wisely refrained from speaking aloud.

By now some of the crowd had dispersed, but those remaining gathered around, though the great-cat at Marleon's side kept them from closing in. But they were calling out questions:

"What are you doing?"

"Who are you?" a woman wanted to know.

"Where did those great-cats come from?" an older woman asked in a quavering voice.

A man called out, "You young'uns need to clear out of the way so we can get a clear shot off at that big cat."

"I'd like the pelt of that one that's down, once it's certain he's good and dead," another said.

"You have some power over that cat, boy?" a man called out to Marleon.

"No, but I'm not afraid of him," Marleon called back.

*Oh, Marleon, you should be,* Serollyn thought, but kept the thought to herself. She feared that until Marleon knew for certain that the cat beside him was not his life-guide, he would endanger himself to keep the great-cat safe.

"Those children are crazy," came a voice from the rear of the crowd. "Crazy and dangerous," it went on. The voice sounded familiar.

"Friend of theirs accused them of setting a great-cat

onto her to kill her. Magistrate didn't believe her, but I do." The speaker was pushing his way through the crowd. "Magistrate let 'em go, and sure enough, they sicced a great-cat onto the two landgraves that brought 'em in for trespassing in their hunting preserve. One's dead and the other's badly hurt and maybe going to die."

He reached the front of the crowd. It was Crinston, the magistrate's man, and he had a rifle, either Munck's or Wilder's, Serollyn guessed. "Magistrate Pell won't be so quick to let 'em go this time, I'll wager."

He pointed the rifle at Marleon. "You folks stand back," he called out to the crowd. "I'm gonna shoot, and whether I hit the boy or the cat, I'll get a killer."

Serollyn had judged Crinston a coward, but the gun gave him courage. The crowd backed away, some fleeing to doorways, others shifting about to stand behind Crinston.

*What should we do?* Nestryn sent frantically.

With Tolammy occupied with the fallen great-cat and Dedryc still howling, whatever was to be done had to be done by Nestryn and Serollyn. And Serollyn could see only one thing to do.

*Wait,* she sent to Nestryn.

# 16

# GUNSHOTS

Neither Nestryn nor Serollyn moved. Dedryc fell silent, but he, too, remained rooted by Nestryn. Tolammy, unseen by all except Serollyn and Nestryn, continued to minister to the great-cat.

Marleon placed himself between the other great-cat and Crinston, just as Serollyn had been sure he would.

"Boy, I'm telling you, I'll shoot you if you don't move away from that cat. I mean to shoot it, but I got no qualms about taking you out first." Crinston leveled his rifle, aiming it squarely at Marleon.

Marleon didn't budge.

Serollyn watched Crinston closely. She had begun to understand something of how the guns worked and intended to time her action carefully. When he pulled back the hammer, she lunged for Marleon, caught him around the knees, and toppled him to the ground. The gun fired. The bullet struck the great-cat, tearing deep into its side.

Serollyn held tight to Marleon's legs, preventing him from rising. She mindsent, *That cat isn't your life-guide. It's the Death Stealers' Sneak. Your life-guide is the other one. Tolammy's trying to keep it alive.*

Marleon stopped struggling against her hold and lay

still. Serollyn was able to look up and see Crinston fumbling with a pouch that must hold powder for his gun. Though she still little understood how the guns worked, she'd observed that he'd need several minutes to get the rifle ready to fire again.

She rose to her feet, and he swung the barrel of his gun around and pointed it directly at her. Meeting her gaze, he said, "I'm aiming for *you* this time, missy."

He was bluffing; he hadn't finished loading the rifle. "You'd be smarter to finish off the great-cat," she said.

The cat had fallen and was thrashing around, roaring in pain. Marleon rolled out of its way to keep from being clawed. He staggered to his feet and looked at Serollyn, and in his eyes she read the question he could not send: *Are you sure?*

"Oh, I'll finish off both cats, don't you worry about that," he said. "But you're a troublemaker, and I'm going to get you first."

"I'll get the cats," said a voice, and the man appeared who'd threatened them earlier with the smaller gun. With its shorter barrel, his gun fit into his hand far too comfortably for Serollyn. He took aim at the thrashing cat and fired at its head, putting an end to its writhing.

Crinston didn't seem happy for the help. "I coulda handled that," he muttered.

The man shrugged. "The cat could've caused a lot of carnage before you did." He drew a second gun from the pocket of his jacket. "You'd be wise to get rid of that rifle and carry a pair of pistols as I do."

He took aim not at Serollyn but at the wounded cat. He must have realized it wasn't dead.

While Crinston was distracted by his anger, Dedryc

launched himself at him and snatched the rifle from his hands. The other gunman swung around in surprise, Marleon leaped at him and hurled him to the ground, where they rolled around, fighting for possession of the short-barreled gun he'd called a pistol.

The crowd, which had scattered at the first shot, regathered and shouted threats. It would only be a matter of time before someone else appeared with a gun. Serollyn left Dedryc and Nestryn to handle Crinston and threw herself into the struggle between Marleon and the other man, her attack enabling Marleon to grab the gun, rise, and train it on the man. Marleon had no idea how to shoot it, but the man couldn't know that.

They needed to get off the street into a place of greater safety. But how could they go anywhere with an injured great-cat to transport?

The great-cat let out a rumbling moan and rolled to rest on its knees, toppling Tolammy onto the ground. Nestryn rushed to her life-guide and picked him up. Her actions had to puzzle the onlookers, to whom Tolammy was invisible. She cradled the monkey in her arms and stepped out of the way as the great-cat attempted to rise.

Marleon handed Serollyn the pistol and jumped to help the cat. He placed his arms under its chest and helped it lift itself to its feet. It stood unsteadily, leaning against Marleon's legs. "I'm sorry," Marleon said. "I should have been able to tell you two apart, and I couldn't."

The cat rubbed against Marleon in a sign of forgiveness.

But why didn't he mindsend? And why couldn't Marleon, if he truly had a life-guide now? Doubt about the cat still filled Serollyn's mind.

Tolammy could answer the questions, but he seemed to be unconscious. Had he been hurt when the great-cat rose, or was he merely exhausted from the work of healing? No time to find out. If the cat could walk, they had to get away. She held the gun in none-too-steady hands, aiming it at its owner as best she knew how. She hadn't spared a glance at Crinston to see how Dedryc was coping with him. Now Dedryc sidled up to her.

"Get rid of that one," he whispered, nodding toward the unknown man on whom she was holding the gun. "That one," he said, pointing the barrel of the gun at Crinston, probably knows where your dog is—and Feryn."

The boy was being clever for once, but how was she to do what he suggested? Even if she could operate the gun, she did not want to kill anyone.

The throng had thinned out, but those who remained were easing closer again. One young boy darted forward and stopped in front of Marleon.

"Is that cat really yours?" he asked.

"In a way," Marleon answered cautiously. "It's not a good idea to come so close to him, though."

The boy backed off only a few steps. Afraid he would get between her and the men she was watching, Serollyn said, "You need to go back to your parents, or whoever you're here with. We don't want anyone hurt."

"I want to help you," the boy said. "See that building over there?"

He pointed, but Serollyn did not dare look; she could not take her eyes off Crinston and the other man she held at gunpoint. "What about it?" she asked.

"It's a holy house. If you can get inside it, no one will go in to haul you out. You'll be safe."

Nestryn came up beside Serollyn. "It might be worth a try," she said. "I need to tend to Tolammy, and Marleon's great-cat can't go very far."

"Can it go even that far?" Serollyn asked.

"He'll try," Marleon answered. "We can't stay here."

The boy might be leading them into a trap. But they had to do something. "Take us there," Serollyn said.

The boy nodded. He backed away in the direction he had pointed, careful not to move in front of the guns or to get between them and the two men from whom they'd taken the guns. That disposed Serollyn to believe him.

"You come with us," she ordered Crinston. To the other man she said, "We wish you no harm. Please stand out of our way, and when we get past, you're free to go."

The man moved to one side, with Dedryc keeping trained on him the rifle he'd appropriated, and she motioned Crinston to walk in front of her. Fortunately, Crinston was a coward and did as she ordered, making no attempt to retake the gun. Nestryn walked beside Marleon, who kept his hand on the great-cat's back. They proceeded slowly, the great-cat leaning against Marleon. Dedryc, walking backward and menacing the crowd with his gun, came last.

The building to which the boy directed them was not especially remarkable. Its stone front was plain except for a plaque above a wide, open doorway. Symbols were carved on the plaque, but Serollyn had no idea what they represented.

A streetlight illuminated the area in front of the building, and as the boy passed directly under the light, Serollyn saw on his shoulder the shadowy form of a moon rat. It was so insubstantial that she would have doubted her senses, except that the creature turned its eyes on her, and in the lamplight their opalescent gleam was unmistakable.

"You have a life-guide," she cried out to the boy.

He looked puzzled. "Don't know what you're talking about," he said.

"Your moon rat. It's on your shoulder."

"A rat? Ugh. There's nothing on my shoulder." He patted the empty shoulder and then the one on which the rat sat. His hand went through the translucent creature.

The ghost of a life-guide? Or one trying to form? Serollyn had never seen such an oddity. She was quite sure she was the only one who saw it now. No one else they'd seen in this place had had a life-guide. If this boy did, she didn't want to lose him.

"Come in with us," she said.

"Better not."

She guessed she'd frightened him by talking of a moon rat on his shoulder. "Please, just see us inside," she begged.

"Yes, show us this isn't a trap," Nestryn put in, misinterpreting Serollyn's motive.

"It's not," he insisted. "All right, look, I'll go inside, and you follow me. Then I gotta go home."

Serollyn nodded. Once she got him inside, if this wasn't a trap, she'd explore the mystery of the moon rat.

The boy passed through the open doorway, walked on for several paces, then turned and beckoned them in.

"Let's go," Marleon said. "Radic needs to lie down."

Serollyn prodded Crinston with the barrel of the gun. "You first," she said.

# 17

# GLIMMER

The building's dark interior heightened Serollyn's fears. But a light flared, and a moment later a candle flame provided a small but reassuring illumination. The boy who'd led them into the building held the candle aloft, letting them see that no enemy was lying in wait.

The doors to the street remained open, and some of the crowd gathered outside, but none entered. It seemed the boy had told the truth.

They drew together in the center of the room, and the great-cat sank down with what sounded like a sigh of relief. Marleon knelt beside it, stroking its side. Nestryn still held Tolammy, so it was up to Serollyn to keep an eye on Crinston and keep the gun aimed at him. Dedryc turned to watch those at the door. Serollyn, not daring to look away from Crinston, asked Dedryc, "Is the other man gone, the one you took the gun from?"

"Don't see him out there anywhere," Dedryc reported. "Should I shut the doors?"

"Yes. We'll be safer," she said. The doors' large wooden panels screeched as they slid along tracks set into the floor. The doors must not have been moved in a while. Dedryc grunted with the effort of pushing first one and then the other until with a clunk they met in the center and shut out the curious gazes of the people outside.

The boy who'd brought them moved around the room, using the first candle to light other candles and place them in candleholders set on small tables arranged at intervals along the side walls. Soon their surroundings became visible. The dark wood-paneled walls were polished to a sheen that reflected the candlelight but were bare of any decoration. The floor was also of wood, clean but not so well polished. Besides the small tables, the room held one long table at the front, away from the door. After lighting a single large candle on that table, the boy returned to them.

"There now," he said, "you're safe and you have light. I've got to leave."

"Wait," Serollyn said, determined to explore the matter of the partly visible life-guide. "Thanks for your help. But what's your name? And do you live near here?"

The boy hesitated as if unsure whether to impart the information, but finally said, "My name's Lorry. I live two streets down from here. And I need to get home."

"Your parents will be worried about you, I guess."

"My parents are dead." He gave the information with a reluctance that was more than sadness. Serollyn sensed anger there, and fear. "I live with my aunt and uncle. They don't want me coming to this place."

"Why not? You said it was a holy place."

"It was holy to the old gods," Lorry explained. "No one worships them anymore. But they still protect this place and anyone who comes in here to be safe. Nobody can come in to hurt or arrest somebody who's taken refuge here. If they do, they'll be stopped."

"Stopped how?" Nestryn asked.

Lorry shrugged. "Just—stopped."

"The place is haunted," Crinston said. "It's full of evil spirits."

"They aren't evil," Lorry said. "They're the old gods, and this is the only place left to them, so they defend it."

"Who taught you that nonsense?" Crinston asked scornfully.

"My parents taught me, and it isn't nonsense. They took care of this place until they—they died."

He'd been going to say something else, Serollyn was certain. Maybe, "They were killed."

"So, your parents followed the old gods?" Nestryn asked.

Lorry nodded.

"Who keeps this place up now?" Serollyn asked. "It looks like it's cleaned regularly."

"I do," Lorry said in a low voice. "My aunt and uncle forbid me to come here, but I sneak in whenever I can and clean the floor and make sure there are candles on all the tables."

"Little fool," Crinston muttered.

Serollyn found this all very interesting, but it wasn't helping locate Krannel. Yet she felt compelled to solve the mystery of the barely visible moon rat that still occupied Lorry's shoulder.

"The old gods, what were they called?" she asked, hit with a sudden suspicion.

"I don't think they had names," was Lorry's evasive answer.

"Well, how did your parents refer to them? Just 'the old gods,' or did they call them something as a group?"

"They called them the—" He stopped as though fearful of saying more.

"The Life Lenders?" Marleon supplied.

Lorry turned to him and nodded.

"So that's why you came to help us, to bring us here," Marleon went on. "Because you knew this great-cat wasn't just an animal."

Lorry looked at the floor. "I didn't know," he mumbled. "Just guessed maybe it could be something more."

"You guessed right," Marleon said. "He's my life-guide."

"And you have a life-guide, too," Serollyn said, grasping the opportunity. "I can see it. I can see other people's life-guides."

Crinston snorted.

"It's true," Serollyn said, responding to the unspoken doubt written on Lorry's face. "I see yours. It's a moon rat. That's not like a plain house rat. It's a beautiful animal. It has long, silver fur that's soft to touch and gleams in the moonlight, and its eyes are silver, too, like the moons. That's why it's called moon rat."

As she spoke, she gazed at the creature, and it seemed to gain substance from her words. She approached Lorry and put out her hand, wondering if she dare try to touch the delicate creature.

"If it's there, why can't I see it?" Lorry asked.

"I don't know. We go through a ritual to get our guides. Maybe it's just that you haven't done that. Did your parents have life-guides, do you know?"

"I ... I think maybe they did," he said. "I heard them talking sometimes when they didn't know I was listening. I didn't understand, but they said something about it

142

being too dangerous for me and they shouldn't tell me, and if one came, it would come. I asked them what they were talking about, and they wouldn't say. They just told me I wasn't meant to hear that, and to forget about it."

"We can teach him the ritual," Marleon said. "But we don't have the things here he'd need."

"The ritual's for calling a life-guide," Nestryn said. "If he already has a life-guide as Serollyn says, he just needs to hear and see it."

"Life-guides talk in your mind," Serollyn explained. "You should be able to hear your moon rat mindspeak to you. It would tell you its name and let you mindsend to it."

A strange expression came over Lorry's face. "I thought … I thought it was a dream," he said. "I kept hearing … I'm not sure what. But at night, when I'm in bed and almost asleep, I hear a word sometimes, repeated over and over."

"What is the word?" Serollyn asked.

"Glimmer."

"That must be its name," Serollyn said, excited. "And what a good name for a moon rat!"

"Not 'it'," Lorry said, catching the excitement. "'She.' It was a girl's voice."

"Speak to her," Serollyn said. "Even though you don't know how to mindsend yet. Just speak out loud, and see if you get an answer."

The moon rat's nose twitched. Her tail curled up over her back, and her head turned to gaze into Lorry's face.

"Glimmer, can you speak to me? Oh! Oh, I see her!" He stared open-mouthed at the small face so near his own.

Glimmer solidified—that was the only word Serollyn

had for it. She had been becoming more visible, less transparent, but when Lorry spoke her name, she lost all transparency and acquired substance.

She lifted a dainty paw and patted Lorry's face. He reacted with a squeal of delight.

*I have been waiting so long,* she sent, and Serollyn heard.

Lorry had heard, too. "I'm sorry," he said. "I didn't know."

*You should have been taught. And now you will be. You must stay with these people and let them help you. And you must help them.*

"Help them? How?" He turned to Serollyn. "I did help you, didn't I? By bringing you here?"

"Yes, you probably saved our lives," she said.

He nodded and turned to the others. "Look at Glimmer," he said. "Isn't she beautiful?"

"We can hear her, but we can't see her," Nestryn said gently. "Most people can't see other people's life-guides. We don't know why Serollyn can, but it has something to do with her life-guide. He's special. Everyone can see him, and she can see everyone's life-guide."

Lorry frowned and looked around, puzzled. "Where is your life-guide?" he asked Serollyn. "Is it the great-cat? I thought that was his." He pointed at Marleon.

"It is," Serollyn said. "My life-guide is a dog, a large yellow dog. He's missing. I think someone took him, and I think this man may know where they took him." She indicated Crinston. "I've got toget him back—and I will."

"You're crazy, all of you," he said. "Life-guides. Old gods. Holy place. Nonsense, all of it. I don't know where your stupid dog is. You should have tied him up."

"A yellow dog, kind of skinny with black smudges on

144

his sides and a black-tipped tail? I saw him." Lorry was jumping up and down with excitement, forcing Glimmer to cling to his shoulders with all four paws to keep from being bounced off.

"Yes, yes! Where did you see him?" Serollyn's excitement matched his.

"Two men were pulling him in a wheeled cage. One said he was a mad dog, but he didn't act like i He just sat real quiet in the bottom of the cage and looked sad."

*Ah, so that's why they were able to get away so quickly.*

"Tolammy! You're awake." In her excitement Serollyn spoke out loud. Seeing Lorry's perplexity, she said, "Tolammy is Nestryn's life-guide. He's a monkey."

"I can't see him, but I heard him," Lorry said.

So Marleon and Nestry were not the only ones who could hear other life-guides. The thought reminded Serollyn to ask, "What about the great-cat, Tolammy? Is he really Radic? Is he Marleon's life-guide?"

*That is a question for Marleon to ask him when he wakes. He is still weak and must sleep for a while, as I had to do after giving him so much of my energy. But he will recover and help us reach Krannel. Now, while we're in a safe place, we should all rest. Dedryc is already asleep despite his concern for Feryn.*

"The way he was howling after the great-cats fought, I thought maybe he sensed something happening to Feryn."

*I believe he sensed the Sneak and feared falling under his power again. Of course he feared for Feryn as well.*

"Do you know where Feryn is?"

*No, but I think he is not far from here. He may have found his way to Krannel.*

Ignoring her exhaustion, Serollyn said, "We have to find them."

*It is too dangerous now. Wait and rest and recover your strength. Let me recover more of mine, and let the great-cat recover his. Remember, I warned you when you defeated the Sneak the first time that he would return. He did, and in a larger, stronger, more dangerous form. We must expect that when he returns the third time, he will be still more formidable. We have a little time before that happens, but he returned this time sooner than I'd anticipated, and he may do so again. We must be ready, which means rested and at our top strength.*

*Also, Lorry needs more time with his life-guide. He must learn to mindsend and will with a bit more time. I know it is hard to wait,* he added as Serollyn went to the door and peered outside. *I will not deny that Krannel is in danger, but so long as Crinston is here with you, the danger is less.*

*Then we must be certain that Crinston doesn't get away while we're all asleep,* Serollyn mindsent. *One of us must stay awake and keep guard.*

"I will," Marleon said. "I want to watch over Radic, anyway." He walked to where Dedryc was curled up on the floor asleep and gently took the rifle from his hands. "I'll keep this with me."

*You should take turns,* Tolammy said. *Let Marleon keep watch for two hours, then I'll wake Nestryn and let her watch, and then Serollyn will take the last watch.*

They agreed to this plan. Serollyn handed the pistol to Marleon for safekeeping. She curled up on the hard wood floor, her pack for a pillow, and was asleep in seconds despite her worry for Krannel and for Feryn.

The hand shaking her awake seemed a part of the dream she'd been having, but Nestryn kept repeating her name until Serollyn understood she was being summoned for her turn at watch. She'd slept through Marleon's

146

watch and Nestryn's. She rose, and Marleon handed her the rifle, keeping the pistol.

Serollyn rose and made a circuit of the room to bring herself more fully awake, assured herself that Crinston was asleep, and settled by the door to keep watch until dawn, the rifle in her hands. Yawning, she wondered how she'd manage to stay awake with everyone else asleep. She did nearly nod off, when she felt a soft nuzzle and jerked upright to see Glimmer beside her.

*Lorry's asleep,* Glimmer sent. *I thought we might talk.*

*It's good you came,* Serollyn sent in return. *I almost fell asleep.*

*It is strange that you can see me, and you told us you can see all life-guides and that everyone can see yours.*

*That's right,* Serollyn said. *And you are the first life-guide I've seen with any of the people here on this side of the forest. Can you tell me why that is?*

*The people have forsaken their devotion to the Life Lenders. This place is the last that holds the memory of the Life Lenders and their connection to all life. The links are broken, and the life-guides cannot come.*

*Links?* Serollyn asked. *You mean the links connecting all life?*

*That's right.* Glimmer's nose twitched in excited approval. *You were taught that all life is linked, and all creatures are interdependent, but these people either were never taught or have rejected the teaching. They think themselves separate from all other life and superior to it. That attitude leads to the enslavement of animals that are useful to them and to the hunting and killing of wild animals for sport. Under such circumstances, life-guides that might have come to them languish and die instead.*

*We met two such hunters,* Serollyn said, thinking of Munck and Wilder. *They were cruel men, and I'd hoped they weren't examples of the rest of the people here.*

*I fear for the most part they are,* Glimmer sent, her tail drooping in sadness.

*But how is it that you came to Lorry?* Serollyn asked, eager to have her curiosity satisfied. Perhaps because Glimmer had for so long been forced to remain silent, she was now happy to talk and more willing to explain things than Tollamy was and than Krannel had been.

*Lorry's mother and father were the last faithful ones,* Glimmer told her. *They taught Lorry their belief in the Life Lenders, though he was very young. They cared for this place and guarded it against desecration. And they begged the Life Lenders to send Lorry a life-guide. But he was only five years old when they were killed, too young at that time to understand all they'd tried to teach him. He was put into the care of his aunt and uncle, who taught him that his parents' beliefs were wrong and that he must not follow them. They never convinced him of that, but they did confuse him. Yet, as he grew older, he came here as often as he dared. Here he feels close to his parents. In recent years he has kept the place clean and kept candles on the tables, candles purchased from his own meager allowance. His aunt and uncle beat him when they find that he has come here, but he does not let the beatings deter him. He comes despite the risk to himself. For that the Life Lenders honored him by sending me. But until you came, I could not make him aware of my presence, and so I was fading away. It was not merely that he did not know the ritual; the ritual is not important. It was that he knew so little about the Life Lenders themselves, though he reveres life as his parents taught him. He must be taught.*

*I helped him see and hear you*, Serollyn said, *but I didn't teach him anything. There wasn't time.*

*That is true*, Glimmer responded. *But you set an example. That is the best teaching. Through watching you and your friends he will learn more about the interrelatedness of all life than he would learn in years of schooling.*

Those words pleased Serollyn, but they also made her think of her flight from her home and the reason for it.

*When Krannel, my life-guide, came, I could see and hear other life-guides, and I saw that many of my people lied about having life-guides.* She paused, gathering her thoughts. *Marleon convinced me that my life was in danger and I was willing to flee because those who lied and those who so easily believed the lies disgusted me. I'm afraid that my people might become like these here on this side of the forest. I don't want that.*

*You have learned wisdom, Serollyn,* Glimmer sent. *If your people lose awareness of the linkage, no more life-guides will come to them.*

*I have to do something!* Still holding the gun, Serollyn rose and walked around to relieve her distress. *I have to go back and warn them.*

*Perhaps that is what you were brought here to discover,* Glimmer said.

Dedryc sat up and looked around sleepily. "Is it time yet to go find Feryn?"

"Not yet," Serollyn whispered. "It's still dark. We have to wait until after dawn. Go back to sleep."

"I had a bad dream," he said, not following her example in keeping his voice down. "I dreamed the great-cat was tearing Feryn apart. I want to know he's all right."

"We all do," she assured him.

"He must be scared," Dedryc said. "And hurting

maybe. Nobody's there to help him. I need to find him." He got to his feet and headed for the door.

Casting a quick glance at Crinston to be sure he was still asleep, Serollyn set the rifle down on the floor and hurried to intercept Dedryc. She reached him as he was struggling with the sliding doors and stopped him from slipping through the narrow opening he'd made by sliding one door back only a short distance.

"Wait," she told him, holding his arms. "In just a short while we'll all go to find Feryn, and Krannel, too."

He struggled in her grasp, and she was giving her full attention to preventing his escape when a menacing growl from the great-cat caught her attention. She realized her danger just in time to duck the blow Crinston aimed at her head with the stock of the gun. She pulled Dedryc down with her, so the blow missed Dedryc and only grazed the top of her head.

Crinston was raising the gun for another blow when the great-cat pounced. It toppled him to the floor at Serollyn's feet where he lay face down, the cat sprawled on his back. Serollyn bent and retrieved the rifle.

"Don't kill him," she begged the cat. "We need him to help us find Feryn and Krannel."

"I wonder if he understands," Nestryn mused, having been wakened by all the tumult.

The cat looked up and growled.

"Of course he understands," Marleon said.

Everyone was now awake, even Lorry, who was sitting up, rubbing his eyes, and turning to stare at his moon rat as if to assure himself that he hadn't dreamed her.

"But I don't know why he doesn't mindsend," Marleon added.

A deep voice rang in Serollyn's mind. *I've kept silence to punish you a bit.*

Marleon gave a glad cry and rushed to his life-guide's side. "Radic! You do send! Why were you punishing me?"

*For not seeing me for so long, after waiting and wishing for my coming,* the great-cat answered. *I've been at your side for some time, but when the Sneak came, you mistook it for me even after it killed a man. You should know that life-guides protect without killing.*

"That other cat was the Sneak?" Marleon looked stricken.

*As you should have known when it killed one man and left another badly injured.*

So either Wilder or Munck had survived. As Serollyn recalled the scene, she thought Munck must be the survivor. Wilder had been too badly mauled.

She had been taught but had forgotten that a life-guide would not kill a person. No wonder she had been reluctant to accept the first great-cat as Marleon's life-guide!

Marleon looked shame-faced. He'd had the same teaching as Serollyn. So had Nestryn. Yet none of them had realized the significance of Wilder's death.

*We're all guilty,* she sent.

*Yes, but you are forgiven. You redeemed yourself by helping Lorry see his life-guide and communicate with her.*

"I'm sorry, Radic." Marleon said. "You're right. I should have known."

*Radic is not my name,* the great-cat sent. *That is the name you gave to a lie. My true name is Delk. It is your ignorance of that name that has kept you from mindspeaking.*

"Delk," Marleon repeated, rolling the word around on his tongue as though tasting it. "Delk."

"Why aren't we looking for Feryn?" Dedryc asked, oblivious to the drama of Delk's revelations.

No one answered. Their attention focused on Delk.

"You gonna let this animal kill me like he killed Wilder?" Crinston whined. "Get him off me, please!"

Delk growled but stayed where he was.

"He won't kill you. He's a life-guide," Marleon said. "It was the other cat that attacked your friends."

"Don't know how you know that," Crinston groused. "Can't tell 'em apart."

Marleon didn't answer. Serollyn knew he'd be embarrassed to admit he hadn't been able to tell them apart, hadn't known which great-cat was his life-guide.

"Come on, enough of this 'life-guide' stuff. The cat's a killer. Call him off. You have the gun. You know I can't hurt you."

"I know you'll try if you get the chance," Serollyn said. "And I'm certain you know more about Krannel's disappearance than you've told us. I believe you contacted someone and either arranged to have him taken away or at the very least knew that he would be taken."

"That's nonsense. Why would I do that? I don't even like dogs."

"Maybe that's why," Serollyn said. "Or maybe you knew he wasn't just a dog."

"You're crazy. That's what I know."

Delk snarled and bared his teeth. His claws tore through Crinston's shirt and dug into his back.

"Ow! He's going to kill me." He let out a scream. "Get him off me and I'll tell you what I know."

"All right, but I warn you," Serollyn said, "if you lie to us, our life-guides will know."

Marleon and Nestryn hauled him to his feet. As Serollyn had suspected, he'd suffered only a few scratches.

Serollyn glared at him. "Now tell us about Krannel."

"Well, you're right. I did send a servant to tell someone to come and get him. His rightful owner. See, I recognized him soon as I saw him. He's a dog that belongs to a friend of mine. My friend was training him to hunt, but the first time he took him into the forest and turned him loose, the dog ran off. Jode searched for him, even set his other dogs to hunt him, but the dog never turned up. Until you showed up with him."

"It's not true!" Serollyn burst out. "You're either lying or your mistaken."

"I'm not lying, and I'm not mistaken. The dog has distinctive markings. I'd know them anywhere—all yellow except for the black muzzle and a black streak down either side. His owner said that coloring would be good camouflage in the woods. That's why he was so mad about losing him. Though I never did think he'd make a good hunting dog. Never wanted to come when Jode called him. Jode'd beat him, but I never saw that it did any good."

"Beat him!" Serollyn was aghast. "I've got to find him. Where is he?"

"I don't know. I doubt he'd take him home."

"Two men had him when I saw him," Lorry reminded Serollyn.

"That's right! Who was with this Jode?"

"Well, if you really did see him, I'd guess it was Jode's brother, San. Big fat guy?"

Lorry nodded. "One was, yes."

"That's San. He eats too much of his own cooking. He runs a restaurant—the one crazy Joxie works at, the woman that mutters about life-guides. Funny coincidence, that."

Was it a coincidence? First the name, Joxie. Now the claim that this Joxie "mutters about life-guides." Surely the woman could only be her mother, Joxlyn. Serollyn had to find out.

"You'll show us where this restaurant is," she ordered. "After we find Krannel."

"And Feryn," Dedryc put in. "We need to be finding him now."

*The boy is right,* Tolammy sent. *We must waste no more time.*

They gathered at the front doors, there being no rear exit that they could find. Serollyn told Dedryc to ease the door open.

He slid one panel open but quickly yanked it shut again. "Men with guns out there," he said.

# 18

# LOSS

"You waited too late," Dedryc wailed. "Now you gotta do something so we can get out and find Feryn."

Serollyn felt the same urgent need to find Krannel, but she didn't see how they could leave.

*Ask him how many "men with guns" he saw,* Tolammy sent.

Serollyn relayed the question.

"Not sure," Dedryc said. "Five or six."

"Must be the City Guard," Lorry said. "They won't come inside after us, but they'll keep watch until we have to come out or starve."

Serollyn realized Dedryc had only a glimpse, so his estimate could be way off. But it was all they had to go on. Their shelter was windowless.

*I have a plan,* Tolammy sent. *Like your Krannel, Delk can be seen by everyone, but Glimmer and I cannot. If you can open the door just wide enough for us to slip outside, I think we can create enough of a distraction to keep the guardsmen busy and give you a chance to escape.*

*I can help with that even though they can see me,* Delk sent.

*If you get shot, you'll be of no use. You can help, but not until we say it's safe for you to come out.*

Nestryn was nervous about having Tolammy go outside without her, and Lorry was distraught at having to be separated from Glimmer so soon after discovering her. But the two life-guides assured their charges that their plan could work and was the only chance they had. Reluctantly, Nestryn assented and, finally, so did Lorry.

They had to explain to Dedryc, who could not receive the mindspeech, what was afoot. He enthusiastically endorsed the plan, and from a position behind the door, slid it open the distance Serollyn recommended and closed it except for a narrow opening when she told him the life-guides were outside.

Serollyn peeked cautiously through the small gap, putting herself at risk to keep an eye on the two life-guides. Since there was room for only one person at a time to view the outside events and she was the only one who could see both Tolammy and Glimmer, she had to relate what was happening.

"I count five guardsmen," Serollyn reported. "They're arranged in a semicircle around the door. They're armed with the long guns, the rifles. Glimmer's climbed onto Tolammy's back. Tolammy took a running leap and is hanging on to the barrel of one man's gun—the man in the center. His weight is pulling the gun down. The man looks scared. He can't figure out what's happening.

"Glimmer jumped from Tolammy's shoulder onto the barrel of the next man's gun. She doesn't weigh much, so the gun just bobbed a bit. That was enough to make the man nervous. Now she's jumping from that gun to the arm of the man on the end of the row.

"Hah! She bit his hand. You should see him jump. He would have shaken her off, but she'd already jumped off him, onto the shoulder of another man. What's she doing? Oh, that's wonderful! She's grabbing hold of his hair and pulling herself up on top of his head."

"She's great!" Lorry exclaimed, applauding wildly until Serollyn motioned him to silence so she could continue.

"The guard's yelling and trying to get her off. Tolammy jumped onto the guard on the other side of the one in the center and is unbuttoning his jacket. Glimmer just leaped from the one guard's head over to the one in the center. I think that one's the leader. He was yelling for order, but now he's trying to grab Glimmer."

"Oh, Glimmer, be careful!" Lorry said.

"She will be. Tolammy will look after her," Nestryn reassured him, slipping an arm around his shoulder.

"Good," Serollyn went on. "He got careless, and Tolammy grabbed his rifle and tossed it toward our door. The guard knocked Glimmer off onto the ground." At Lorry's worried gasp, she hurried to add, "She's not hurt. She ran to the fifth man and is biting his ankles. While they're keeping the men distracted, I think I can open the door enough to get the gun."

She pushed the door open a little farther and, watching carefully, chose the right moment to reach out, grab the gun, and duck back in with it.

A moment later Tolammy tossed another gun within her reach. Although the squad leader yelled for the men to reclaim the guns, the two disarmed guards had had enough; they turned and ran. Another soon followed.

Tolammy and Glimmer concentrated their efforts on the two remaining guardsmen, biting them, tearing their clothes, never letting them get a grip on their tormentors. Serollyn chuckled as she described their antics. While the leader swatted wildly at the place Glimmer had been, Tolammy vaulted upward, grabbed hold of the man's belt, and unfastened it, then swung aside to avoid the man's frantic grabs. Glimmer caught hold of one pant leg with her teeth and Tolammy yanked on the other, and the guardsman's pants slid off. Serollyn's chuckles turned to howls of laughter. The man snatched at his trousers, only to have either Tolammy or Glimmer bite his fingers. The others joined in the laughter as she described the scene.

The fourth guardsman, seeing his leader's struggle with the invisible enemies, took off running after his comrades. Their leader, abandoned by his men, stepped out of his trousers, and in short white pants he'd worn beneath the trousers he ran off after the deserters.

*Now,* Tolammy sent, *it's safe for everyone to come out.*

When the group left the building, they saw that not only had the guardsmen run away, but onlookers who had gathered to watch the excitement had also fled.

Serollyn still held a rifle and used it to prod Crinston into motion, but she no longer worried about how to fire it. There seemed little likelihood that the need would arise. Marleon walked beside her carrying the pistol, and Delk stalked next to Crinston, snarling at him often to keep him unsettled. Tolammy had reclaimed his place on Nestryn's shoulder, and Glimmer rode on Lorry's.

Along the street shops were open, and vendors hawked their wares to shoppers who wandered from store to store. One look at Delk and the citizens gave Serollyn and her friends a wide berth, ducking into stores or running in the opposite direction.

Dedryc walked beside Serollyn. "How we gonna find Feryn?" he prodded.

"Tolammy knows where they took Krannel," she said. "He'll lead us there. He thinks we may find Feryn with Krannel."

"I don't know why you're taking me with you," Crinston groused, keeping a wary eye on the gun Serollyn held. "I've told you all I know about the stupid dog. He's with his rightful owner. You'd do best to forget about him."

Serollyn tightened her grip on the gun and hoped she looked like she knew how to use it, though she feared she didn't fool him. "No matter what you say, Krannel is my life-guide, and I intend to get him back. I may need to exchange you for him."

"Exchange a man for a dog? Girl, you're crazier than that Joxie woman."

"Maybe so," Serollyn said. "Or maybe neither of us is crazy. I'm mean to go and see Joxie as soon as I get Krannel back."

"And Feryn," Dedryc put in. "Don't forget Feryn."

"We're not forgetting him," Nestryn said, giving the boy a hug. "We'll find him."

*We're nearing the building I traced Krannel to,* Tolammy sent as they reached an intersection. Dedryc lurched to the right. "Feryn!" he shouted and broke into a run.

"He must sense him," Marleon said. "I don't see him."

It seemed to Serollyn that if Dedryc could sense Feryn, she ought to sense Krannel. She tried mindsending and thought she felt, rather than heard, a wisp of a response. She said nothing to the others because she was unsure she had truly felt it and not merely wished it.

Delk loped easily after Dedryc; the others ran along behind, trusting Delk not to lose the boy. The street narrowed and passed between buildings old and in disrepair, many looking abandoned. The decay was more than physical deterioration. Serollyn sensed a miasma of evil pervading the section.

Dedryc came to a sudden halt, and the others skidded to a stop behind him.

"What is it?" Marleon asked.

Dedryc didn't answer but turned in a slow circle, sniffing the air as though he thought he could scent Feryn. Serollyn again tried a sending to Krannel.

*That is the building to which I traced him,* Tolammy sent, indicating a hulking brick building with boarded windows. *I sense that he is here but cannot respond. Let me scout around while the rest of you stay here. This is a foul place.*

He leaped from Nestryn's shoulder and was gone before she could voice an objection. She sighed. "Why does Tolammy always insist in putting himself in danger?"

*That is his responsibility as a life-guide,* Delk sent.

Tolammy returned sooner than anyone expected. *The building is not locked and they are both inside, but there is grave danger,* he announced. *A trap has been set there for us. If we enter, we may not leave alive, and a rescue for both may not be possible.*

"Explain," Marleon said. "Who else is in there?"

*At the moment, no one.*

Dedryc gave a cry and headed off toward the building.

*Stop him!* Tolammy sent.

Delk leaped after him and grasped his arm in his mouth, holding him until Marleon and Nestryn could grab him and drag him back to the middle of the street. Dedryc howled as he had when the great-cats fought.

*Does that mean the Sneak is back?* Serollyn sent.

*I'm not sure,* Tolammy responded. *I don't sense it, but it may be able to hide its presence.*

"Well, we can't stand out here dithering," Marleon said. "We've got to take a look. With Delk here, and Crinston as hostage, we ought to have a fair chance."

*You don't understand the situation yet, but I think you'll have to see for yourselves,* Tolammy sent. *Heed this warning: Keep hold of Dedryc, and don't touch anything at all inside. Especially not Krannel or Feryn.*

When he led them into the building, Serollyn understood the reason for those instructions.

The interior was a large, empty space, dusty and foul smelling. Krannel and Feryn were its only occupants. Krannel, bound with chains, lay on a table next to a post. Above him hung a steel blade positioned to decapitate him if it fell. From the blade a rope went through a pulley and down to wrap around Feryn. Unbinding Feryn would release the rope and drop the blade on Krannel.

From Krannel's bindings another rope was tied through a complex series of pulleys to drop down from them and encircle Feryn's neck. Studying the arrangement of ropes, chains, and pulleys, Serollyn saw that freeing Krannel would strangle Feryn and freeing Feryn would decapitate Krannel.

Feryn was unconscious. Dedryc wanted to go to him, and Nestryn and Serollyn had to hold him back while Marleon examined the deadly setup.

Crinston burst into laughter. "Someone's left you quite a conundrum," he said.

Delk snarled and snapped at him, the powerful jaws brushing Crinston's arm. Crinston jumped back. "Call him off!"

"He acts on his own," Marleon said. "He's my life-guide, not a trained animal."

"And I'll bet you know who set this trap," Serollyn said, turning to him without releasing her grip on Dedryc. "And you probably also know how to free Krannel and Feryn without either being killed."

He shrugged, still grinning. "I don't know either thing, but I can see that there's no way of freeing them without the death of one or the other."

"That can't be so," Serollyn insisted. "There has to be a way."

Marleon stood under the rope, chain, and pulley system, studying it carefully, using his index finger to try to trace the discrete parts of the confusing network.

Serollyn turned away from Crinston in disgust and tried to communicate with Krannel. Her life-guide was conscious; his eyes were open and gazing at her with a sadness she had never seen there before. But he did not mindsend, nor did he in any way acknowledge her sendings.

Delk stalked back and forth from Marleon to Serollyn to Crinston. Tolammy leapt from Nestryn's shoulder to Marleon's and joined Marleon in trying to visually disentangle the deadly confusion above them.

Lorry, with Glimmer on his shoulder, prowled around the perimeter of the room, occasionally kicking at something or picking it up to examine it: a small block of wood, a short length of frayed rope, a bit of broken glass. Serollyn noticed that after examining one such object, he slipped it into his pocket. But he was too far from her and too much in shadow for her to know what the object was.

When Lorry completed his circuit of the room, he

returned to Marleon. "Glimmer can gnaw through ropes. She thinks she's light enough to climb the chain without making the blade fall. Once she gets up there," he indicated the web of crisscrossing ropes and chains, "she'll be able to tell which goes to what and how to unlink them so you can free the dog and that boy."

Crinston gave a derisive snort. But the plan seemed sound to Serollyn, and she was glad to hear Marleon agree to it. She watched Glimmer scamper up the chain from the blade to the first pulley, touch it lightly with one paw, then leap over it to land on two crossing ropes. The whole precarious contraption shuddered slightly, but the blade did not move, and so far as Serollyn could tell, the rope around Feryn's neck grew no more taut.

Glimmer clambered over and under the system of ropes. *This is truly evil,* she sent. *I can see no rope I can gnaw through without harming one or the other or both.*

The hope that had blossomed with Lorry's suggestion turned to a lead weight in Serollyn's chest. Glimmer had to be wrong; there had to be a way. She released Dedryc's arm and drew near Krannel to see whether she and Marleon could get beneath the blade and hold it in place while Nestryn and Dedryc freed Feryn. But the steel blade was long and heavy and sharper than any knife Serollyn had seen. They would not be able to get a grip on it and prevent it from slicing through their hands as it fell.

Dedryc broke away from Nestryn and ran to Feryn. Nestryn raced after him.

*Don't be afraid.* The sending from Krannel came unexpectedly. *I will always be your life-guide.*

Tolammy leaped onto Dedryc and bit at his hands to wrest from them the noose around Feryn's neck.

Dedryc persisted despite Tolammy's efforts. The noose slipped from around Feryn's head. The blade descended. Serollyn screamed. Streaming blood, the head of a yellow dog rolled onto the floor.

*The Death Stealers have won for now,* Tolammy sent sadly.

# 19

# FOUND

Voices bombarded Serollyn's ears, but the words made no sense to her. Someone's arms went around her, held her close.

Somewhere someone was crying. Someone wailed over and over the words, "I'm sorry. I'm sorry. I didn't mean to kill him." The words should make sense to her, she knew, but she couldn't make sense out of them.

"Take her outside," someone said.

"We need to find a place to bury the body."

What body? What were they talking about?

"Feryn's alive. He's breathing. But I can't wake him."

"I'll carry him. We need to get away from here."

"We can't just walk off and leave Krannel like that."

"Where's Crinston?"

"He ran out. With so much happening, I couldn't stop him. He took the rifle Serollyn dropped."

"Let him go. We shouldn't have brought him."

The arms that had held her released her, and another arm slipped around her shoulders and guided her outside. When she felt the sunlight against her face, she opened her eyes and looked around.

It was Nestryn's arm that hugged her shoulders. Lorry

stood beside Nestryn looking worried. Marleon carried Feryn in his arms. Dedryc hovered close to Feryn, begging him to wake.

Serollyn blinked. Awareness returned, and with it a wash of grief. She cried out, "Krannel!" and crumpled to the ground.

Nestryn knelt beside her. "Shhh," Nestryn soothed. "I know. It's terrible, I know. There was no way we could stop it."

"But Krannel," Serollyn managed before breaking into loud sobs. "He can't be dead. He's a life-guide. He can't …"

Silence except for her own sobs. Then Nestryn said, "Tolammy's right, you know. We mustn't stay here."

More silence until Nestryn said, "So is Glimmer. Come on, let me help you up." She rose and helped Serollyn to her feet.

Serollyn looked around. "Right about what? Where is Tolammy?"

"Right here," Nestryn said, turning to the side so Serollyn could see her other shoulder. "Right here on my shoulder."

Serollyn looked, then turned to look at Lorry. "Where's Glimmer?" she asked him.

"Here," Lorry said, raising his hands toward her, palms up.

Serollyn shook her head. "No," she moaned. "Oh, no!"

"You can't see them?" Nestryn asked.

"Or hear them." Serollyn burst into fresh tears.

"Can you see Delk?" Marleon asked, coming nearer.

Serollyn was afraid to look. Nestryn put her hands on either side of Serollyn's face and gently turned it toward Marleon.

Dedryc moved aside without meeting her gaze. Delk stepped between Dedryc and Marleon and stared up into her face.

"Yes! Yes, I can still see Delk." Her excitement died as quickly as it had arisen. "But everyone can see Delk. Just like everyone could see Krannel."

"Can you hear him?" Marleon asked.

She waited. Nothing. He must be sending, and the others heard, but in her mind there was only an unbearable silence.

Devastated, she walked away from the others. They had witnessed her disgrace. They hadn't saved Krannel. Dedryc had acted rashly and no one had stopped him. She had to be alone to grieve and to cope with the terrible emptiness of being cut off not only from Krannel but from the other life-guides she had seen and spoken with and counted as her friends.

Marleon caught up with her and put his arms around her. She didn't want his comfort. She pushed him away. "Go back to Feryn." She started to run.

He ran after her, caught her, and held her again. "Feryn's all right," he said. "Nestryn is caring for him. You need me more than he does."

She needed to be alone. Why couldn't he understand?

"Then go back to Delk," she said, struggling to free herself again. "He can talk to you."

"Look, Serollyn, I know how you must feel. I understand that you want to be alone. But it's too dangerous for you to go off on your own. We don't know where Crinston went. We don't know who set that trap that killed Krannel and almost killed Feryn and would have if Glimmer hadn't chewed through the rope that was strangling him. Because the plan was clearly to kill them both."

"So someone wants to kill me," she snapped. "Isn't that what you told me to get me to come on this fool's quest? Isn't that what started this whole mess, and now Krannel's dead, and I have no life-guide—just like Vali. Just like you until Delk came. And someone's still trying to kill me. Are you satisfied?"

He stared at her, shocked. She knew how deeply she hurt him and how unjust her attack had been. She didn't care. Her pain and grief demanded that she strike out at someone. Anyone. And Marleon was at hand.

Her vitriol should have driven him away, but it didn't. His only response was to hold her tighter, pressing her against him. "You need to cry," he told her. "You'll feel better if you do."

She shook her head, rubbing it across his shoulder. She did not want to cry; she wanted to scream and vent her anger to the world. To the Life Lenders. She'd served them faithfully, and they'd done this to her. Where was their justice? Their fairness?

She might have said all those things aloud, had her face not been pressed too tightly into the crook of Marleon's neck.

"You can't fall apart on us, Serollyn," he murmured into her ear. "You are our strength. Our wisdom."

She shook her head again, her lips brushing against the bare skin above his wraparound. "That's Nestryn," she said, her voice muffled. "And you. I'm just a girl who sees—saw—other people's life-guides. Now that's gone."

He smoothed her hair. "You're more than that," he said. "Much more than that to me."

His tenderness reached her at last. This was a side of Marleon he'd only let her glimpse until now. Now, when she didn't want to see it. When she wanted to cling to her blind rage. Instead, her arms slid around his waist, and she clung to him and sobbed.

"That's right," he said. "Cry it out."

It took a long while. But when the sobbing subsided, she did feel better. "I'm sorry," she said. "I didn't mean those things."

"I know. Forget it."

"I guess we should go see how Feryn is." She eased away from him, and this time he didn't try to hold her back. He took her hand and led her toward where the rest waited for them.

She stopped before reaching them. "I need to know something first," she said. And in answer to his questioning look she added, "I need to know whether I can still mindsend."

"Maybe you should wait," he began, but stopped abruptly.

*You're kinder to me than I deserve,* she'd sent. *I love you for it.*

She wasn't certain whether she'd meant the message just for Marleon or for them all. Certainly they'd all been patient with her.

She didn't expect the answer she got: *I love you, Serollyn.*

She stared at Marleon and saw his face turn red.

"You can send now!" She squeezed his hand.

"I didn't know … I wouldn't … I didn't mean …"

"It's all right, Marleon. I'm just happy for you that you can send—and happy for me that I heard."

They walked rapidly to where the others waited. Still embarrassed, Marleon said, "I'll go in and see about getting Krannel's body and burying it. Don't watch, Serollyn."

She nodded and turned away from the door to the building. "How's Feryn?" she asked, not ready to think about Marleon's inadvertent sending.

"Breathing better, but still unconscious," Nestryn said.

"We saved him," Dedryc said so proudly that she wondered whether he'd already forgotten that his rash act had cost Krannel's life.

But Dedryc hung his head and added, "I'm sorry about Krannel. I didn't know ..." His voice trailed off.

She swallowed the lump that rose in her throat and tried to sound normal. "I know you didn't mean for Krannel to be killed. You were concerned about Feryn."

Marleon exited the building looking puzzled.

"He's gone," he said. "Krannel's body is gone. There's nothing to bury."

They all had to troop back into the building to see for themselves, Serollyn leading. It was true. The table on which Krannel's body had lain held the chains that had bound him, the blade that had severed his head sunk into the wooden tabletop. The floor where his head had fallen was empty even of the blood that had spilled from his neck.

"Who could have taken him?" Marleon asked.

"No one," Serollyn answered firmly. "It means he's not dead."

"Serollyn, you know that he is," Nestryn said gently. "That blade cut off his head. We all saw it."

"Yes, but he's a life-guide. Somehow he'll come back.

I'll see him, I know I will." She reinforced that conviction with a mental plea: *Krannel, I need you. Come back, please. I know you can't be truly dead.*

"We'd better get away from here," Marleon said, giving no indication of whether he'd heard her mental plea to Krannel. He gathered Feryn up into his arms and led the way down the street, Delk at his side.

"Lorry, do you have any idea where we'll be safe?" Marleon asked as he marched along.

"No, but I found this in that place." He dug into his pocket, pulled out a crumpled bit of paper, and held it out for inspection. "It might mean something."

"What is it?" Marleon asked, looking mystified.

"It's a sales slip," said Lorry, interpreting the markings on the paper. "From a diner called San's place."

"San's place!" Serollyn exclaimed, staring at the paper. "San's one of the men who took Krannel away. His place is where they said a woman works who talks about life-guides. Do you know where it is?"

Lorry nodded. "It's not far from here. I can take you there. Glimmer says I should."

"Then let's go," Serollyn said.

They retraced their steps toward the area of newer, finer buildings. Here men and women filled the streets, but no one seemed to be hunting them. Everyone they passed took one look at Delk and stepped quickly well out of their way. Serollyn did hear mutters of "witch children" and "killers" from some, a warning that they weren't out of danger. Marleon had the pistol stuck in the band beside his knife.

She concentrated on trying to mindsend and succeeded at last at picking up a faint sending from Tolammy.

*Tolammy, I can hear you! Thanks be to the Life Lenders!*

*You never lost the power to hear or send,* he responded. *You suffered a severe shock that closed your mind to our sendings. It is not an unexpected reaction.*

Not unexpected! But how many people lose their life-guides?

She had not sent the thought, but Tolammy picked up on it. *Krannel was especially vulnerable,* he said. *As is Delk. He's already had a close brush with death.*

A glint of silver on Lorry's shoulder distracted Serollyn. She concentrated, and the glint took on a nebulous shape. Glimmer! As she stared, she began to make out details. The moon rat was curled on Lorry's shoulder, sleeping, her tail twitching a bit as if in a dream.

She turned to look at Nestryn and laughed to see an indistinct brown form on her friend's shoulder. *Tolammy, I can see you again!* she sent.

*Shh! You'll wake Glimmer,* Lorry mindspoke.

*Good for you!* came from Marleon.

Good, yes. Good to see the other life-guides. But it didn't heal the hurt at Krannel's loss. It emphasized his absence.

Seeing Tolammy perched on Nestryn's shoulder, one paw resting on her head, and Glimmer riding on Lorry's shoulder, her eyes closed, her head against his neck, seeing Delk stalk proudly at Marleon's side, only made her more aware of the void at her side where a yellow dog should be, tail wagging, ears alert.

Although he'd been late in coming to her, she felt that Krannel had always been at her side. And nothing could ever fill the emptiness there.

"San's place is just ahead," Lorry announced, pointing.

The place he indicated was an old building with a faded sign announcing SAN'S PLACE.EAT HERE.

Serollyn came to a halt in front of the door, both eager and afraid. Finding her mother could not make up for the loss of Krannel, but it would bring her some consolation.

"Please, wait outside until I call for you," she asked her companions. "If this Joxie is my mother, I want to meet her alone."

They seemed to understand and stood aside to allow her to enter. Slowly she pushed the door open and walked in.

In a room with tables covered with faded cloth and scuffed and nicked wooden chairs, an old man and a young boy sat at one table, and three hard-faced men sat at another. In front of the latter were dirty plates. They must have just finished their meal. The other tables were unoccupied. Serollyn saw no one else in the room.

A door swung open, and a woman came out carrying a tray laden with plates of food. The woman's dark hair was heavily streaked with gray, and deep lines carved her face, but Serollyn knew her.

She had found her mother.

## 20

# JOXLYN

Serollyn stood quietly, observing the woman, though her heart was thumping in her chest like a caged animal fighting to free itself. Her mother had not so much as glanced her way. her gaze was fixed on the table where the man and boy sat. She set the tray down and placed the plates of food in front of the diners, all the while moving her lips as though muttering to herself. The young boy snickered, earning a stern look from the older man.

"Talking to your life-guide again, Joxlyn?" one of the three diners said.

She shook her head, and Serollyn moved nearer to hear her mother's response.

"Don't have a life-guide, not any more," her mother said. "Had one, but it died."

The light in the diner was dim, but Serollyn saw something that was not a shadow on her mother's shoulder. She drew nearer.

Yes, it was there! A bird, its feathers dirty and drooping, its head tucked beneath its wing. She recalled that her mother's life-guide had been a magnificent white tern. Serollyn had been only four years old when her father was killed in the hunting accident and her grieving mother disappeared into the forest. Her memories of her parents were vague. But she did recall her mother speaking proudly of her life-guide and describing how the pure white feathers gleamed in the sunlight. She searched her memory for the bird's name.

She recalled finding the name difficult to say. Her mother had laughed at her attempts and gently corrected her. She tried to call forth that name as her mother had pronounced it, slowly and distinctly, encouraging Serollyn to repeat it after her syllable by syllable.

*Mi-*. It had started with *Mi*. She couldn't remember the rest, but she was sure it would come.

Her mother had finished serving the customers and looked up to see her. With no sign of recognition, she said, "Would you like to be seated and order?"

Not trusting herself to speak, Serollyn nodded.

Her mother indicated a table near the one she had just served, and Serollyn took a seat. Joxlyn pointed to a board with markings Serollyn couldn't read, though she pretended to study it.

"I'll be back to take your order," her mother said, and began filling her tray with the soiled dishes from the table where the three men sat. One of them stuffed coins into her pocket.

"That's for you, Joxie," he said. "Put the meals on my account."

"San will have to okay that," she said. "I'll get him."

"My credit's good," the man said, and all three rose to leave.

"San doesn't like me taking credit." She headed toward the kitchen door. As soon as she disappeared through it, the men hurried from the diner.

Serollyn followed them. "Stop those men," she called to Marleon and Nestryn. "It *is* my mother, and they're trying to cheat her."

Marleon sped after them, Delk loping beside him. Serollyn returned to her table, confident that the men would soon be brought back. She was right; the three men stumbled through the door, followed closely by Marleon and Delk.

"Sit down," Marleon said. "The lady will tell you what you owe, and you'll pay."

The men glanced nervously at the great-cat, but one spoke defiantly. "Lady, hah! That's just crazy Joxie. She don't know nothin'."

Marleon glanced questioningly at Serollyn, who rose from her seat at the table.

*She hasn't recognized me,* Serollyn sent. *I'm sure those men planned to cheat her.*

The door to the kitchen swung open and a man emerged, so wide he had to squeeze through the door. Once through, he barreled toward the three men Marleon had trapped, his face purple with rage and exertion.

"Trying to weasel out of payment, are you? Taking advantage of poor Joxie, here. We'll see about that." He grabbed the man who'd spoken for the others, twisted him around by his arm, which he pulled so high and tightly against the man's back that Serollyn heard a bone snap.

The man let out a howl of pain.

"You'll pay me what you owe me for today and all the times before," San said.

The man nodded and, while San kept his hold on one arm, dug into his pocket with the other and came up with a fistful of coins. His companions did the same, and they all poured the coins into San's free hand. Several rolled off onto the floor, and the men bent to retrieve them, giving San a clear view of Delk, behind them.

"What in the name of the gods is *that?*" He demanded, staring at the great-cat.

"He's Delk, sir," Marleon said. "And he's keeping these men from running out without satisfying their obligation to you."

"Tame, is he?"

"No, sir. He's my life-guide."

The big man, who had to be San, groaned. "Not another one!" he said. "Joxie here is always nattering on about life-guides and how she lost hers. Didn't know she was talking about a great-cat."

"She wasn't," Serollyn put in. "Her life-guide is a bird, a white tern. And he's not lost."

At that, Joxie took notice of Serollyn again. She sidled around the men and stood directly in front of Serollyn, peering into her face. Scarcely daring to breathe, Serollyn let her mother examine her.

"Not lost, no. Dead," she mumbled, more to herself than to Serollyn. "Died long ago."

"Are you confusing your life-guide with your husband?" Serollyn asked. "I know he was killed in a hunting accident, but your life-guide is right there on your shoulder."

Her mother shook her head violently, then peered even more closely into Serollyn's face. "How do you know these things?" she asked.

"Don't you know me, Mother? I'm your daughter. I'm Serollyn."

San waddled over to them, having evidently been

satisfied with his payment and Marleon and Delk having let the men go. "Her daughter!" he said, scowling at Serollyn. "You aren't playing with poor Joxie, are you?"

"Her name is Joxlyn, and she is my mother," Serollyn said. "She disappeared after my father was killed in a hunting accident. I've been searching for her."

"Hmm. I do see a resemblance between you," San said. "Tell you what. You and your friend and his cat did me a favor. You sit down at that table and get re-acquainted with your mother, and I'll fetch food for you and your friend, and the great-cat, too."

"Sir," Marleon said, "That's very kind of you, and we are hungry, but we have no way of paying, and we have several other friends outside, including a boy who's ill."

"By the moons, I'm not running a hospital or a charity feeding station," San said. "But tell your friends to come in. I'll see what I can do. No more animals, are there?"

"No, sir," Marleon said. In response to Serollyn's sharp look he sent, *There're none that he can see, and they aren't animals. They're life-guides.*

*He helped capture Krannel,* Serollyn sent. *We can't trust him.*

*We don't know that he was responsible for setting the trap that killed Krannel,* Marleon sent. *He seems friendly now.*

*Maybe. Tell the others to come in, but warn them to be careful.*

As Marleon went to follow her instructions, Serollyn grasped her mother's hands and led her to a seat at the table where she'd been sitting before.

"No, no. I can't sit," her mother objected, eyes darting about. "I have to take orders and bring the food."

"No, mother. He said you could sit and talk to me.

Come, now. Sit down. Relax."

She sat opposite Serollyn, but she did not relax. Serollyn had to grasp her hands to keep her from jumping up when Nestryn, Lorry, and the twins came in. To Serollyn's relief, Feryn was awake and stumbling along, held up by Nestryn on one side and Dedryc on the other.

Through all that had happened, the man and boy who had been served just after Serollyn arrived had continued to eat. Now the boy jumped up. "Lorry," he called. "Lorry, what are you doing here?"

Lorry and the boy greeted each other, and Lorry was invited to share the table with the boy and the man, who was introduced as the boy's grandfather. Nestryn, Marleon, and the twins settled themselves at another table, with Delk settled on the floor beside Marleon.

Serollyn called her mother's attention to Marleon and Nestryn. "You remember them, don't you, mother?" she asked. "We all played together when we were little."

"Marleon. Nestryn," her mother repeated the names. "Can they really be almost grown? Can you?"

"So you know me now?"

At last her mother met her gaze with the light of sanity in her eyes. "Know you? Of course. I couldn't forget my daughter. How is Corlon?"

Serollyn's heart flooded with relief. Her mother not only knew her, but remembered her brother. "He's fine, Mother. He's married to Laki, Kinnin's daughter."

"Laki … Laki." Her mother rolled the name around on her tongue. "Pretty little girl. I remember."

"Not so little any more." Serollyn laughed. "But they're happy and doing well. They have a five-year-old son named Vannon."

She would have said more, but at that moment San trundled out, pushing a cart loaded with food. "You're all my guests," he boomed. Serollyn did notice that his eyes narrowed as his gaze fell on Dedryc and Feryn. Or was it her imagination? He acted genuinely enthusiastic as he went on, "And not just because of how you dealt with those sneak thieves. No, you're friends of Joxie, family even, and that merits a celebration."

He piled food on all three tables, including his two customers in the bounty. "Enjoy!" he said, and returned to the kitchen.

Perhaps Marleon was right, and San had not been the one who'd set the trap. More likely it was Jode, the man who, according to Crinston, claimed to be Krannel's owner. She'd ask San about it later, but for now Serollyn decided to ignore her suspicions and focus her attention on her mother. She could see that her companions were all hungry and eager to eat.

"You eat, too, Mother," Serollyn urged. "You look like you haven't been taking care of yourself."

"I work hard," her mother said, not picking up her fork. "It's all I have left."

Serollyn had to reach through her mother's wall of self-pity. She left her own food untouched to say, "No, Mother. You have me. You have Corlon and Laki, and your grandson, Vannon. And you do still have your life-guide. What is her name?" Serollyn had recalled that the life-guide was female.

Joxlyn shook her head sadly. "I told you, Mirivell died long ago, right after I ran into the forest. I've been without her as long as I've been here."

Mirivell. Yes! Serollyn remembered the name now.

She looked at the tern still perched on Joxlyn's shoulder. The bird looked ill, but it was certainly not dead.

She launched a tentative sending toward the bird: *Mirivell, it's Serollyn. Can you hear me? Please wake up. I must understand why my mother can't see you or sense your presence.*

A sending came back, but not from Mirivell. It was an urgent message from Tolammy.

*Serollyn, don't touch the food. Look around you. You've been tricked.*

She had been ignoring her friends at the other tables. Now she looked around and gasped in dismay. Marleon sat slumped over, his hand lying limply in the food remaining on his plate. Dedryc had fallen forward into his plate of food. Nestryn was sitting upright, but looked glassy-eyed and unaware. Tolammy tried in vain to rouse her. Feryn slid silently to the floor.

At the other table Lorry and his friend were both asleep, and the friend's grandfather was shaking his grandson and moaning feebly. Glimmer scampered frantically around the table, trying to wake Lorry.

Delk stood on shaky legs, gagging and retching.

*So far as I can tell, the food holds only a sleeping draught,* Tolammy sent. *Except for what was given to Delk. That was poisoned, but he ate only a small bit. If he can regurgitate it, he should be all right. But you are in terrible danger. Don't eat and don't let your mother eat.*

Serollyn looked back at her mother, who was stirring her fork in her food. She raised the fork to her mouth. Serollyn leaned across the table and slapped it from her mother's hand. Her mother gave a frightened cry and backed her chair from the table.

"He's drugged the food, mother," Serollyn said quickly.

"Look around."

Her mother gazed around, her eyes growing wide in alarm. "No," she moaned. "I should have guessed. He's not given to kindness."

San chose that moment to reappear from the kitchen. He glanced at the three tables and scowled to see Serollyn and her mother still awake and alert.

"Joxie, get back to the kitchen at once," he ordered.

But Serollyn caught her hand and kept her from obeying. "She's not your slave," she told the big man.

"Little fool, I'm trying to protect her," he said, no trace of joviality left. "I've sent for the city guards. They'll be here at any time. If your mother's in the back, she won't be involved."

"And you won't be without a serving woman, is that it?" Serollyn snapped.

He smirked. "That too."

"I should do as he says," her mother said, pulling away.

"No! Stay here," Serollyn said so forcefully that her mother sank back into her chair.

"So you'd put your own mother in danger to protect yourself," San said. "You can't escape. Your friends are all unconscious and likely to stay that way for some time— long enough for them to be carted to a secure cell."

But they weren't all unconscious. *Tolammy, Glimmer, I'll need your help. And Delk's if he can manage. And Mirivell's. She's got to wake up.*

*To wake her, your mother must mindcall to her,* Tolammy sent back.

*Mother, can you hear me?* Serollyn sent desperately.

Her mother gave no indication that she heard. She'd have to speak aloud. She cast an anxious glance out the front window. No city guards had yet arrived. Maybe San was bluffing, but she doubted it.

"Mother, listen to me." She caught her mother's gaze and held it. "I can see life-guides—anyone's life-guides. I don't know why that gift was given to me, but it was. And I see Mirivell very clearly. She's sleeping on your shoulder. She looks ill because you've neglected her, but she isn't gone and she isn't dead. I can't wake her, but you can, and you must. I need her help, and so do you."

San's eyes narrowed and he bore down on Serollyn, his fists clenched, his fat face flushed with rage. "You're as crazy as she is," he snarled, "but we're going to put an end to that craziness."

He grabbed at her but backed off when Delk snarled. Delk might not have recovered enough to launch an attack, but she was grateful for any support he could give.

Mother, hear me, please, she sent. *My life depends on it. Hear me and mindspeak to Mirivell.*

Her mother shook her head, not in negation but as if to shake off an annoying fly.

*You do hear me, but you're resisting. Do you want me to be killed? Please, please, let me through. And call Mirivell.*

A whisper touched her mind, tentative and frightened. *Mirivell?*

Serollyn watched the tern, saw it shift its weight slightly and withdraw its head partway from under its wing.

*Call her again, Mother. She's responding.*

*Mirivell?* The whisper was louder, but still filled with fear and doubt. And San plodded toward the door, alerting Serollyn that the city guards were arriving. Time was running out.

183

The tern lifted her head from beneath her wing and shook her feathers. She leaned over and gave Joxlyn's cheek a hard peck.

"Mirivell! You live!" Her mother's delighted outcry was followed by the opening of the outer door to admit a bevy of guards. They tramped in and were greeted by San, who conferred in whispers with the leader.

Taking advantage of the momentary reprieve, Serollyn sent, *Delk! You have to wake Marleon. And Tolammy, wake Nestryn.* She would have sent the same message to Glimmer about Lorry, but she doubted that the boy would be of much use in a battle, and he might be safer if he slept through it. She did not intend to let the guards take her and her friends without putting up a fight.

But Tolammy sent, *We are trying. But even if Marleon and Nestryn wake, what can you do against so many armed men? You can't fight your way out of this; you have to talk your way out. And now would be a good time to begin.*

A guardsman aimed his gun at Delk. "No!" Serollyn screamed and jumped in front of the great-cat.

"Move aside, Girl, before I shoot you, too," the guardsman said, glaring at her.

"Why do you want to shoot the great-cat?" she asked.

"He's a killer, that's why," the squad leader put in.

"He's not a killer," Serollyn said. "The other great-cat was the killer, the one that was shot earlier."

"Now how would you know that?" the guardsman said sarcastically. "One great-cat don't look much different from another. And it don't matter anyhow: one's as bad as another."

"That's not true," Serollyn said. "This one's not wild. He's, ah, trained."

It pained her to refer to a life-guide as a trained animal, but that was something these people might understand.

"You telling me it's a pet?" the leader asked.

"I guess you could say that," she said.

Tolammy advised, *Don't just spar with him. Go on the offensive.*

She put her hands on her hips and said, "I don't understand why you've all rushed in here like this. My friends and I have done nothing wrong. But this man," she indicated San, "has drugged our food, and he tried to poison the great-cat."

"Look, I don't know what game you're playing, little girl, but I've never heard of a tame great-cat, and I doubt that you have, either."

Nestryn stirred and groaned.

"Look, another one's coming around," San said. "You're wasting time. Take care of 'em now while most of 'em are still unconscious. I tell you, they're dangerous, even if they are just kids."

"I don't know why you say that." Serollyn stepped forward, though careful to remain in front of Delk. "We came in here peaceably, and we stopped those men from cheating you. Is this how you repay us?"

"You came in here upsetting my serving woman and keeping her from doing her work," San retorted.

"Your serving woman is my mother," Serollyn snapped.

"Crazy Joxie?" one of the guardsmen said, and burst out laughing.

Joxlyn stepped up beside Serollyn. "You may think it funny, but Serollyn is my daughter, and she's come a long

185

way to find me. She's done nothing wrong, and neither have her friends. I don't understand why San sent for you."

"You don't understand anything, ever," San said. "Just stay out of this."

"I don't like the way you speak to my mother," Serollyn said. "And I certainly don't care for the way my friends and I have been treated. I demand to see the magistrate."

That demand produced a flurry of whispers as the guards and San conferred. San was gesticulating furiously, but apparently he failed to get his way. The leader of the group of guards looked at Serollyn. "You've appealed to the magistrate, have you? Well, then, that's where you'll go. But I warn you: keep that great-cat under tight control or it *will* be shot."

## 21

# TRIAL

The guards had to wait until all had regained consciousness before they could escort the group to the magistrate's house. The delay made the guards angrier and more impatient. Serollyn kept a wary eye on the one who'd wanted to shoot Delk. The great-cat lay quietly by Marleon, showing no sign of hostility even when a guardsman took Marleon's gun and knife.

Marleon and Nestryn were the first to wake, followed by Lorry. Their life-guides no doubt helped them recover.

Marleon seemed alert, Nestryn only a little less so, but Lorry was still woozy, and Dedryc and Feryn could barely stand. Marleon and Serollyn had to support them as the guards ushered everyone outside. When Lorry was fully awake, the guards told him that he was free to leave and should return to his home. They seemed to know his aunt and uncle. But he insisted on staying with his friends.

Joxlyn refused to stay behind, and San announced that he was coming, too. "I mean to give testimony," he said and hung a CLOSED sign on the diner door. "Can't do much anyway without a serving woman." He glared at Serollyn.

The guards surrounded them as they trooped through the streets. Passersby gawked and jeered, but the guards prevented any assault and Delk's presence discouraged the curious from pressing in closely.

They reached the building to which Wilder and Munck had conducted them on their arrival in this town. Crinston opened the door and grinned evilly as the guards escorted them into the courtroom where they'd been taken before. Serollyn wondered whether she'd done the right thing in appealing to the magistrate. Magistrate Pell had not treated them unkindly, but Crinston was his man.

As before, the magistrate entered only after they'd all taken seats on the wooden benches before his high desk. He came in through a rear door, and San and the guards stood respectfully as he strode to his place behind the desk. They yanked their prisoners to their feet as well.

Frowning, the magistrate gave them a stern gaze. "I did not expect to see you back here, but I've heard things that have made me regret releasing you." He looked at the leader of the guards. "What are the charges?" he asked.

"Many and serious, Magistrate Pell," the guard leader replied. "Having a dangerous animal that killed Landgrave Wilder and severely wounded Landgrave Munck. Causing a riot in the center of town. Imprisoning and threatening Stalwart Crinston. Disrupting this man's business," he indicated San, "by bringing the great-cat into his diner and terrifying his customers. And resisting arrest."

"The charges are false," Serollyn protested.

She would have said more, but the magistrate ordered her to keep silent until asked to speak. "You'll have your chance to be heard," he said.

Crinston led Vali to a seat near but not with them. Vali did not deign to look toward her former friends but kept her gaze fixed on the magistrate.

Other people filed into the room, people whom Serollyn did not recognize. Lorry glanced back at them and groaned. *My aunt and uncle are here*, he sent.

"I believe more witnesses have arrived," the magistrate said. "Stalwart Crinston will call each of you in proper order. Stalwart?"

Crinston rose from his seat beside Vali. "You have heard this young lady before, Magistrate Pell, but I believe her testimony must be reevaluated in light of the subsequent events. As first witness, I summon Vali."

Vali rose and repeated the charge that the accused had set a great-cat on her in an attempt to kill her. She went on to accuse Serollyn, Nestryn, and Marleon of having stolen two young boys after killing their protector.

Marleon shook his head, his face flushed with anger.

After Vali's lengthy account, Crinston called a witness to the attack on the Landgraves Wilder and Munck. "Landgrave Wilder fought bravely," the man declared. "Even knowing he couldn't win against great-cat, he didn't give up. Not even after the cat had clawed and bit him so blood was pouring out of him. He fought to the death, he did."

Two other witnesses corroborated his account and added details of their own, mostly fictional, of the accused summoning the cat after the Landgraves had overpowered the young man, meaning Marleon, who attacked them with a gun. Still another spoke of seeing them leave the scene of the crime with the great-cat loping along beside them.

"Did they show any fear of the great-cat?" the Magistrate asked that witness.

"No, sir. Quite the opposite. They acted proud of it. I

even heard the fellow there," pointing to Marleon, "praise it for what it did."

Serollyn glanced at Marleon. The testimony was damning. The mixture of truth and lies if accepted would condemn them, though to what punishment she did not know.

Lorry's aunt and uncle spoke next. A portly middle-aged couple, overdressed in Serollyn's opinion, he in dark long-sleeved shirt and trousers, and she in a matching dark, long-sleeved blouse and ankle-length skirt. They looked more like sister and brother than man and wife.

"Our nephew has always been a bit rebellious," the uncle said. "We've had to discipline him frequently for disobeying us. But he never ran away, never stayed away from home, until these youngsters got hold of him. We heard how they took him away with them after the cat fight, and it seems they've kept him with them these two days, whether by force or persuasion I can't say."

"He was always weak-willed," the aunt put in. "Easily led astray, you know. We've had a time keeping him on the strait and narrow. His parents had fed all sorts of foolish notions into him before they came to their deserved end. We've done our best to rid him of their teachings, but he's stubborn, and it hasn't been easy."

"My parents didn't deserve what was done to them," Lorry shouted, jumping to his feet.

"Silence, boy!" the magistrate thundered.

Crinston hurried to Lorry and shoved him back onto the bench. Lorry sat glowering but did not try to speak again. His aunt and uncle gave the Magistrate a triumphant look, as if Lorry's outburst confirmed all they'd said.

At last the parade of witnesses ended. Magistrate Pell peered at Serollyn and her friends. "Who speaks for you?" he asked.

"We'll speak for ourselves," Serollyn said.

The magistrate shook his head. "That is not permitted at this time," he declared.

"You mean we have no right to defend ourselves?" she demanded.

"Your statements will be heard at a later time," he said. "At this time we are hearing witnesses. Who speaks for you?"

At this repetition of his question Joxlyn rose to her feet. "I do," she said.

Titters sounded from the witnesses, and Serollyn heard whispers of "That's crazy Joxie."

Her mother must have heard the whispers, but she did not back down. "I wish to speak for my daughter and her friends," she said.

"And who is your daughter?" the magistrate asked, not bothering to conceal a smile.

"She is," she said, pointing. "Serollyn. She's come a long way to find me."

"Have you proof that this girl is your daughter?"

"Only the resemblance between us," Joxlyn said. "And the fact that she claims me as her mother, as I claim her as my daughter."

"I'm afraid that means nothing. She is not known to be trustworthy, and you have a reputation for speaking nonsense."

"I have been deeply troubled but not mad, as people have labeled me," Joxlyn continued bravely despite the Magistrate's antagonism. "I was grieving the loss of my

husband and the knowledge that his death came because of
something he lied about, a lie I did not know of until after
his death. When I learned of it, I wanted to get away from
the shame he brought on me and my family. I left my
home and my children and came here. Serollyn has
restored my hope and lifted my shame."

"And just how did she do that?" Magistrate Pell asked
too quietly.

"She found me and came to me and made me see my
life-guide. I'd thought my life-guide had left me or died as
I passed through the forest. But she hadn't. She's with me.
In my grief and my anger I couldn't see her, but she's been
here all the time." Joxlyn's eyes filled with tears that
spilled over her lashes and ran down her cheeks. "Serollyn
made me able to see and hear Mirivell again."

Titters and snickers sounded throughout the room,
and Joxlyn must have heard, but she continued bravely.
"For the first time since I came here, I feel I can return to
my home. I owe that to my daughter, Serollyn."

"So your daughter also believes in these supposed life-
guides?" Magistrate Pell asked derisively.

"My daughter knows they are real, and so do her
friends," Joxlyn said.

"Why do we not see these marvelous beings?" the
magistrate asked.

"A life-guide is generally seen only by the one to
whom it is sent," Joxlyn said. "My daughter has the ability
to see all life-guides, though I don't know how she got
that ability."

"Ah, but you cannot see hers?"

Joxlyn admitted that she could not. With a fresh pang
of grief, Serollyn realized that her mother assumed she

had a life-guide. She hadn't had the opportunity to tell Joxlyn about Krannel and how he died.

"Or any but your own?" Magistrate Pell persisted.

"That's right. That's the way it is," Joxlyn said.

"Now let me see if I understand this aright," the magistrate said, peering down at her from his lofty seat. "You can't see any life-guide but the one you claim to have. Others who claim to have these life-guides can see none but their own. Only your daughter can see all these things that are invisible to everyone else, and you and her friends all believe this claim of hers. Is that correct?"

"Life-guides aren't things," Joxlyn declared, ignoring the magistrate's sarcastic question.

"Could you explain what they are, then?" he asked, obviously enjoying this interrogation.

"They look like animals," Joxlyn said. "My Mirivell is a white tern. I don't know what my daughter's is."

Laughter rippled through the room.

The magistrate lifted his little wooden mallet and brought it down sharply on his desk. The laughter subsided.

"So you have not seen the life-guides of your daughter and her friends?" the magistrate inquired.

"No, I can't see any life-guide but my own."

"So you have only your daughter's word and that of her friends that these, ah, guides, exist."

"That is all I need," Joxlyn said.

"You have never seen any life-guide but your own, the white tern? Yet you are willing to swear that all these things—oh, excuse me, these beings, these animals exist."

"I've seen Marleon's life-guide," Joxlyn said.

"May I see it?" The magistrate's lip curled.

"Yes. He's right there by Marleon."

Delk had been lying quietly beneath the bench where Marleon sat, just behind Marleon's feet. Magistrate Pell had apparently not noticed him. Now he raised his head and peered up at the magistrate.

"You brought a great-cat into my courtroom?" he bellowed, rising from his chair and leaning across his desk to glare at Marleon. "That beast? That killer?"

"A life-guide is not a killer," Marleon defended his guide.

The magistrate ignored him. "Stalwart Crinston, why have you allowed that cat in here to endanger us all? Why has it not been shot?"

Crinston paled. "The guards allowed it in, sir," he said, clearly hoping to evade responsibility.

Marleon was on his feet. "I gave my word Delk would harm no one," he said. "I won't be separated from my life-guide."

"Then you'll be shot as well," the magistrate decreed. "That is your sentence for the killing of Landgrave Wilder."

"He killed no one," Serollyn shouted, jumping up.

"Silence!" thundered the magistrate. Then in a lower voice, he said, "I'm disposed to condemn you all to death. But I will give you one chance to save yourselves. I believe all this business about life-guides is nothing more than a pack of lies. If you can prove otherwise by showing me— no, by showing us all," with a sweep of his hand he included the witnesses and spectators, "letting us see these life-guides you rant about, I will spare you all."

"But that's impossible," Nestryn said, speaking for the first time.

"So I judge," Magistrate Pell said. "Yet I am being fair in giving you the opportunity to prove me wrong and save yourselves."

Serollyn sank back onto the bench. *Tolammy, what can we do?* she sent desperately. *If only Krannel hadn't been killed and everyone could still see him, it might have made a difference, but now …*

*Now he is gone. But you are not without resources.*

*What does that mean?*

She got no answer, but saw Lorry and Marleon watching her as if everything depended on what she did next.

She stood again, slowly this time. Keeping her voice low, she said, "Magistrate Pell, in addition to Delk, there are three other life-guides here: my mother's, Nestryn's, and Lorry's. Dedryc and Feryn do not have life-guides. If you will give me some time, I will attempt to make it possible for you and perhaps others as well to see them."

He stared disbelievingly at her for a moment and then burst into laughter. "Oh, that's a clever ploy, my dear. And how much time would you want? A week? A month? A year?"

She swallowed her fear and said, "No, Magistrate, I ask only for the rest of this day."

"And would you have all these people wait here for the next several hours?"

"No one need wait if they do not wish to do so," she said. "You have heard all the witnesses and pronounced sentence. Let those who wish to leave do so and those who wish to remain may wait. Let me confer with my friends, and I will do what I can."

"What of the great-cat?" Crinston asked.

"He must stay with us," Serollyn said.

"I sense a trick, yet I admit to being intrigued," the magistrate said. "I ask the guards to keep their guns trained on the lot of you. Everyone else may leave if they wish or stay and see this charade to its end if that is their choice. You may have one hour only to confer, after which you must either show me these mysterious life-guides or be taken outside and shot, all of you."

"I accept those terms," Serollyn said.

# 22

# SIGHT

"Serollyn, are you crazy?" Nestryn demanded. "We have no way of making people see life-guides when they don't even know what life-guides are."

"It probably is crazy," Serollyn acknowledged, "but it's the only chance we have."

"But we can't even see each other's life-guides," Nestryn persisted. "I mean, you can, but the rest of us can't."

"Everybody can see Delk," Serollyn said. "And before he was killed, everyone could see Krannel."

"Yes, and no one believed that Krannel was a life-guide, and no one believes that Delk is," Nestryn continued to argue.

"So what's your plan?" Marleon asked quietly.

"I don't have one yet," Serollyn admitted.

Nestryn merely rolled her eyes, while Marleon shook his head, looking disappointed.

They were crowded into a small room behind the large room where the magistrate had held court. In addition to their group, which included Joxlyn, guards were stationed in the doorway with guns trained on them. The guards could hear their conversation, but despite that, Serollyn felt they should speak aloud rather than mindsend, since in that way Dedryc and Feryn could be included. The others had given rather reluctant consent when she pointed out that the twins were frightened enough without being kept in ignorance of what was happening and thus becoming still more frightened.

"Do you have any idea how to proceed?" Nestryn asked caustically.

"Well, first l, there's no more time for riddles. I need to know plainly from Delk why he can be seen and Krannel could, while other life-guides cannot. Except by me. I need to know why I can see them all. Delk?"

*Krannel was a living dog as well as a life-guide. The Life Lenders chose him to be a very special life-guide. They infused him with a Life Lender's own spirit and sent him to you.*

Serollyn frowned, then nodded slowly. "So everyone could see Krannel because he was exactly what he seemed to be. Of course, he was much more than that, but people only knew what they could see. And Delk, that means that you, too, are a living great-cat as well as a life-guide. Which also means that you can be killed as Krannel was."

*I very nearly was killed,* Delk sent. *Tolammy saved me by stanching the flow of blood and at the same time giving me a large portion of his own life force.*

*That should mean that Tolammy and the other life-guides aren't really alive and therefore can't be killed,* Nestryn sent, too deep in thought to speak aloud. *But Tolammy has been injured and near death on more than one occasion.*

*That is because the Death Stealers can destroy us by draining our life force,* Tolammy sent. *What you perceived as physical injuries were injuries of the spirit.*

"This is all very interesting, but it doesn't tell us how

to let the other life-guides be seen," Marleon pointed out.

Serollyn considered. "First, I think Vali should join us. She may not be able to see them, but she knows we have life-guides. That may help us."

"But she's determined to see us put to death," Nestryn objected.

"She's not in her right mind," Marleon said.

"No, Serollyn's right."

Marleon and Nestryn both started when Joxlyn spoke. They had probably forgotten her presence. Serollyn had observed that her mother had a way of fading into the background and remaining unnoticed.

"As children, the four of you—Serollyn, Marleon, Nestryn, and Vali—were inseparable," Joxlyn went on. "There is a bond between you that cannot easily be broken—just as the bond between Mirivell and me was not broken despite my madness and my repudiation of her. Vali is mad, as I was, and has repudiated you, but I do not believe that the bond between you is dissolved."

Serollyn turned to the guards. "You must know who Vali is. Can a couple of you go to her and bring her here? Tell her we can't do this thing without her."

"She won't want to come," one guard said.

"In her heart she knows we aren't guilty," Serollyn said. "Bring her even if she doesn't want to come."

"Don't know as Magistrate Pell will approve," the guard objected.

But a young guard said, "We'll do it. I want to see this thing either happen or not happen. I'm curious."

Two guards detached from the group of six and left the room. They returned in moments with a loudly protesting Vali.

"I want nothing to do with these people!" she shouted.

Before Serollyn could act, Joxlyn went to Vali and put an arm around her. "Vali, dear, I haven't seen you in so long," she said. "I know you're upset, but calm yourself, please. No one means you harm. Remember the good times you all had as children, playing together in my home."

Vali quieted and stared at Joxlyn. Her hostile expression didn't change, but the stiffness went out of her arms and shoulders.

"You used to call me your second mother," Joxlyn continued. "Remember?"

Slowly, Vali nodded.

"I hope you'll still think of me that way," Joxlyn said.

Vali didn't answer.

"Once you tried to pet my Mirivell, even though you couldn't see her. You said then that you did feel her soft feathers. I didn't know whether that was true or not, but let's try again."

Vali made a small grunt of protest and turned in Joxlyn's arms, but did not break free.

"Come, give me your hand," Joxlyn said, reaching for Vali's hand.

Vali allowed Joxlyn to take her hand and lift it to the shoulder on which Mirivell sat, head cocked, waiting. Serollyn held her breath as she watched her mother place Vali's hand on Mirivell's back and move it to stroke the smooth white feathers.

Vali seemed oblivious to the close scrutiny she was being given from everyone in the room. For a moment her face was expressionless, then a tear slipped from the corner of one eye.

"I feel her," she said. "I don't see her."

"Still, you know she is there," Joxlyn said, smiling. "Just pet her a bit."

But she broke away. "No! It's a trick! I don't even know if you really are Serollyn's mother!"

"That's not true." Serollyn fought back tears. They'd come so close! Vali had felt Mirivell. Serollyn was certain of it.

Joxlyn mindsent, *Let Lorry come to me.*

Lorry moved to her side. Joxlyn grasped Vali's hand, placed it in Lorry's, and told Lorry to raise Vali's hand to Glimmer's back. He obeyed, and Vali let out a little squeal.

Her jaw set, she pulled her hand away. "He's not even of our people. What can he know of life-guides? And why should I help you when my life-guide is dead?"

"Vali, that wasn't a life-guide." Serollyn was losing patience along with hope. Their time was almost gone. She'd failed.

"He was," Vali insisted. "More of one than that stupid dog you thought was yours." She looked around. "Where is he, anyway? He run away after all?"

"He's dead!" The words burst from Serollyn, and with them came a flow of tears.

Dedryc eased up beside her and patted her arm.

But Vali said with an air of triumph, "Dead? But a life-guide can't die."

"Then why do you keep accusing us of killing yours?" Marleon demanded in a voice taut with anger.

Again Joxlyn stepped beside Vali and put her arms around her. "You're right. Life-guides can't die. But we can die to them. I did that. For many years I insisted Mirivell was dead because I'd closed my mind to her, refusing to hear or see her. Or feel her. And I suffered terribly because of it. As you're suffering. Punishing yourself, I'd guess. But you have no need to. We're all your friends. We all care about you."

Serollyn had forgotten how kind and gentle her mother could be. And Vali *was* punishing herself; Joxlyn was right—about that, anyway. Life-guides did die. She knew that all too well. About that her mother was wrong, but how she wished she were right!

"This isn't working at all," Nestryn said, despair and sorrow filling her voice.

Marleon, his anger faded, merely shook his head. The life-guides were all strangely silent.

Dedryc and Feryn clung to each other. Dedryc gazed imploringly at Serollyn.

She couldn't give up! They were all depending on her. And though she was angry at Vali, anger was not the answer. She could almost hear Krannel encouraging her to keep trying, to have faith, to be patient.

"Vali," she said, "Mother is right. We do care about you. We want you to go home with us. But none of us will ever get home if you can't admit the truth. That you did touch Mirivell. You felt Lorry's life-guide. You know they are there."

"Well, maybe I did feel something," Vali said grudgingly. "I didn't see anything, though. You can't see life-guides."

"You saw Krannel," Serollyn said in the same even tone. "You see Delk."

"I never thought Krannel was anything but a dog."

"And do you think Delk is nothing more than a great-cat? You yourself called him Marleon's life-guide."

Vali cast an uneasy glance at Delk. "I may have been wrong," she said.

"You were wrong," Marleon said. "Wrong about the great-cat that attacked you. That wasn't Delk. But Delk *is* a life-guide, and he'd never harm you."

Delk rose and rubbed against Vali's legs like a cat. Serollyn expected her to jump away and scream. Instead, she reached down, cautiously placed her hand on his back, and stroked him.

The guards had aimed their guns at Delk when he moved. Now they stared in amazement.

"All right, you win, all of you," Vali said, continuing to stroke the great-cat. Tears flowed freely from her eyes. "They're real. The life-guides. I felt them. I didn't want to admit it. I never had a life-guide of my own."

A weight lifted from Serollyn's heart. Vali had just inadvertently confessed not only her old deception but also her knowledge that the Sneak had not been a life-guide.

Dedryc edged near Delk and Vali. "Can I pet him, too?" he asked.

"Sure," Marleon said. "You know he won't hurt you."

Dedryc stroked the great-cat's side and rubbed his neck.

"I want to pet Tolammy," Feryn said. "Can I?"

Nestryn looked at Serollyn. Serollyn nodded. "Let him try."

Nestryn knelt beside Feryn and placed his hand on Tolammy's arm. Feryn's eyes went wide with wonder. "His fur is so soft!"

Dedryc left off petting Delk and went to his brother. "Let me feel too," he begged.

Nestryn placed his hand on Tolammy's head. He grinned with delight and scratched the monkey's ears.

To the guards the two boys must seem to be stroking what only appeared to them as empty space.

"This is taking too long," Marleon warned. "Our hour is almost up."

"Shhh. We're making progress."

The young guard who'd volunteered to fetch Vali because he was "curious" stepped forward. "Do they really feel something?" he asked. "Do you think I could?"

His fellow guardsmen laughed, though the laughter sounded strained. "It's all an act!" one said.

The young man ignored them and approached Serollyn.

"I think you might be able to," she said. "If you really want it. Nestryn and Tolammy, come here."

Nestryn rose with Tolammy on her shoulder and walked to Serollyn's side, leaving Dedryc and Feryn looking disappointed. Tolammy jumped to the guard's shoulder and placed a paw against the man's chin.

The young guard reached up and placed his hand over Tolammy's paw. "I feel it," he said excitedly. "It's a monkey, isn't it?"

Nestryn told him it was.

He broke into a wide smile. "They *are* real," he exclaimed, turning to his comrades.

Delk stalked silently to Nestryn's side. Dedryc and Feryn followed him, each keeping one hand on the great-cat's back. Casting a worried look at the guards with guns, Marleon hurried to place himself between Delk and the guards. But none raised a gun.

Responding to a sending from Delk, Serollyn told the

young guard to place his other hand on Delk's back. "Don't be afraid," she added. "He won't harm you."

The guard placed his hand on Delk's back, gingerly at first, then more firmly. Standing thus between Nestryn and Delk, Tolammy on his shoulder, Lorry to one side of him, he looked first at Delk and then at Tolammy.

"I see him," he said in an awed voice. "I see the little monkey. And I see the moon rat," he added looking at Glimmer, riding Lorry's shoulder. "I see the bird, too! They've been telling the truth."

Dedryc and Feryn broke out in happy laughter. "So do we," they said in unison. "We see them all."

"So do I," Joxlyn said, joining the laughter. "It's a miracle!"

All the guards crowded into the room, wanting to see the life-guides, too. Serollyn and Marleon had a hard time persuading most of them to wait outside and let one at a time come to touch the guides and try to see them.

Not all succeeded. In addition to the young guard who had started the trend, two others were able to first feel and then see Glimmer and Tolammy. Strangely, they could not see or touch Mirivell, though Vali, Dedryc, Feryn, and the young guard all could.

*Mirivell has not yet recovered her full strength after years of neglect,* Tolammy explained. *I doubt that she'll manage to reveal herself to anyone else today.*

That explanation told Serollyn that it was the life-guides who allowed themselves to be seen, and that it was not easy for them.

*You must all save your strength to let the magistrate see you,* she sent quickly. *He must be convinced.*

She turned toward the guards. "Please let the life-guides rest for the little time we have left of the hour we were given," she pled. "They do not find it easy to make themselves visible, and they must let the magistrate see them."

The guards returned reluctantly to their post at the door and left the group alone to wait to be called back to the hearing room.

The call came too soon. Serollyn very much feared that the life-guides had not had time to regain any strength. But there was no help for it. The guards ushered them all back before Magistrate Pell.

Not many in the audience had remained. Most had left, no doubt certain of the outcome of the hearing.

Magistrate Pell stared down at them, his expression stern. "You've taken the full hour," he said, "and my guess is you've come up with nothing. I certainly see no more than I saw before you went into the conference room."

"Sir, some of the guards have seen our life-guides," Serollyn said.

"And I've seen them," Vali put in. "I want to retract the charges I made against my friends. I was wrong. It was all a misunderstanding, and they have not lied about having life-guides or ... or anything else."

Poor Vali! How difficult and humbling making that admission must have been. Serollyn felt proud of her.

The magistrate stared down at Vali. "I don't understand your change of heart. You should not have been allowed to meet with them; I did not authorize such a meeting. What have they done to persuade you to withdraw your accusations?"

"They reminded me of what close friends we used to be. And they let me see their life-guides."

He shook his head as though he found her statement impossible to believe. Addressing Marleon, he said, "Are you prepared to let me see these life-guides?"

"We are, if you'll come down here to us. You have to touch the life-guides before you can see them."

The magistrate's angry scowl showed his opinion of that suggestion. "I will not put myself at risk," he said. "I will neither venture close to the great-cat nor place myself among you where the guards could not protect me."

"But, sir, if you can't trust us, we can't do what you ask," Marleon said.

"And I won't trust you unless you show me the life-guides, so we seem to be at an impasse, and I have no choice but to pass judgment."

"Wait!" Serollyn called out. "Will you allow me to approach you? If so, I can show you one life-guide, and if you see one, you may then see the others."

Magistrate Pell continued to scowl, and he would certainly have refused, but the young guard spoke up. "Sir, it's a truly wonderful experience, and if the girl alone approaches you, we can protect you from any danger."

Murmurs of "Don't be fooled" arose from the spectators remaining in the hearing room, but the magistrate said, "Very well. Let's put an end to this charade. Young lady, you may come forward."

Tolammy jumped to her shoulder, and Mirivell flew to her other shoulder. The life-guides calmed her fear, and she approached the magistrate.

"I have two life-guides with me," she told him. "My mother's and Nestryn's. I will try to help you see them."

"You'd best do more than try," he said. "This is your last chance to save yourself and your friends."

## 23

# DEATH STEALER

With a silent prayer to the Life Lenders, Serollyn stood beside Magistrate Pell and placed his hand around Tolammy's paw. She held her breath, waiting.

He ran his hand along the monkey's arm, up to his neck and down his back. His expression changed from one of skepticism to puzzlement to awe. Serollyn knew the moment he saw Tolammy. His eyes widened, and his glance swept from Tolammy's nose to his tail. Magistrate Pell drew a sharp breath. "I see him," he said.

She smiled. "Now that you've seen one life-guide, perhaps you can see others," she said.

She would not have included Mirivell, but the bird had flown to her on her own, so Mirivell must feel capable of manifesting at least briefly. She asked Mirivell to flap her wings so that they would brush the magistrate's face. When Mirivell did this, the magistrate raised his hand to his face and then out to touch Mirivell, who'd settled back onto Serollyn's shoulder.

Serollyn heard a commotion in the room behind her, but could not break her concentration to see what was happening.

"You kept your word," the magistrate said. "I didn't

believe you, but I see. I don't understand, but I see. I'm dismissing the charges against you."

"You can't do that!" someone shouted.

Serollyn turned and saw a tall man so thin that he reminded Serollyn of the stick dolls made by the children in her village. His face was all hard angles and his eyes were narrow slits.

"These people killed Landgrave Wilder; have you forgotten?" the man demanded of the magistrate. "Because they've tricked you into thinking you see some mythical creature, will you turn them loose again to wreak more mayhem? Is that what your duty demands of you?"

"My duty demands, sir, that I keep my word," the magistrate said. But Serollyn read indecision in his eyes.

"Then I'll bring fresh charges against them," the man declared. "I charge them—especially that girl," he pointed at Serollyn, "I charge her with theft!"

"Theft, sir?" Magistrate Pell asked. "Theft of what?"

"Of my dog! May I explain?"

Magistrate Pell nodded, but the man was already speaking. "Magistrate Pell, I am Jode Garl, a hunter. A few months back I lost a young dog I was training. I took him into the forest, he ran away, and I never did find him. That is, not until Stalwart Crinston there,"—he pointed to Crinston—"sent a messenger to tell me he'd seen the dog in the company of children Landgraves Munck and Wilder had brought before you. He said the dog had been left outside on the steps. Well, sir, I came to see, and sure enough, there was my dog. He'd grown a bit, but his markings made him easy to recognize. Well, I thought I'd best reclaim my property. The dog didn't want to go with me, but I got my brother San to help me get him into a cage, and we took him to my place. Now maybe these young folks figgered he was a stray dog that it was okay to claim, but they sure knew he didn't belong to them and—"

Serollyn jumped to her feet. "He wasn't yours and he wasn't a dog. Krannel was my life-guide. You killed him!"

"He was no more use to me, that was clear. He'd never make a hunting dog. But I didn't kill him. You or one of your friends did that."

The magistrate pounded on his desk with the wooden mallet, but Serollyn paid him no heed. She saw again Krannel in his last moments regarding her with such sadness and such love—and then the blade falling. The decapitated body, twitching. The blood.

"You set a trap!" she shouted. Turning to Magistrate Pell, she said, "He didn't just take Krannel, he took Feryn." She pointed at the boy, who cringed and nodded in confirmation. Serollyn continued. "He tied them both in such a way that untying Krannel would strangle Feryn and untying Feryn would make a blade fall and ... and cut off Krannel's head. And Feryn's brother didn't know. He ... he untied Feryn, and the blade fell, and ..." She burst into tears. Joxlyn took her into her arms, and she sobbed on her mother's shoulder.

"Is this true?" Magistrate Pell demanded of Jode.

"Sir, we didn't take the boy. He ran into the building where we had the dog. He acted crazy, shouting all kinds of things. We had to tie him to keep him from hurting himself or somebody else. There wasn't any trap, though. That's a lie. I don't know how the dog got killed."

"You're the liar!" Dedryc shouted. "You made it so I'd kill Krannel."

"Look at him and his brother," Jode said with a sneer. "Twins! That's what they are! Everybody knows twins are bad luck and worse. Crazy. Dangerous."

"So you deny setting the trap the young woman described?" Magistrate Pell asked.

"Of course I deny it. The boy wasn't hurt. And the dog was mine. I could do what I wanted with it. What I wanted was to lure these young people into a place where we could catch them and lock them up and bring them to justice. We would have succeeded, San and I, but for that great-cat. Don't you believe for one second that animal isn't vicious."

"He isn't acting vicious," the magistrate observed, looking at the cat lying at Marleon's feet. "And they were telling the truth about their, ah, life-guides. So I am inclined to believe them."

At that, San rose from his seat beside Jode. "Don't forget that these people used the cat to murder Landgrave Wilder and leave Landgrave Munck grievously wounded."

Serollyn recalled the sales slip from San's Diner Lorry had found in the place where Krannel and Feryn were imprisoned. "*You* set that trap!" she accused San. "You're responsible for Krannel's death."

San strode toward Serollyn, his great body shaking the floor with each angry step. An evil glint in his eye awakened a fearsome memory for Serollyn—a sudden vision of the interior of the lair the Sneak had made for himself and the "wood boys." She felt the same sense of wrongness, of a hunger for death. *I think that's the Sneak.*

Tolammy leaped back to Nestryn's shoulder. *You may be correct*, he sent.

"Take your seat and be silent!" Magistrate ordered.

San did not obey. "If you don't intend to render the just verdict for the crime of murder, it's my duty as a citizen to effect justice myself."

Moving with unexpected speed, he grabbed a gun from the hands of the guard who tried to intercept him. He pointed the barrel at Serollyn. Delk let out a menacing growl.

"You have failed to kill this animal," he said. "I'll remedy that, too." San turned the gun toward the great-cat.

"No!" Marleon threw himself in front of Delk.

"No!" Serollyn echoed, diving for the gun.

San swung the gun toward her. In the close quarters he could not miss. As he fired, Joxlyn leaped in front of Serollyn. The rifle ball struck Joxlyn. She fell to the floor, blood pouring from a terrible wound.

The young guard who'd first seen the life-guides fired at San. The fat man toppled next to his victim.

"No," Serollyn screamed, and fell beside her mother. "No, I just found you!"

"And saved me," her mother said, her voice so faint Serollyn could scarcely hear. "I'm proud to die for you. And for your life-guide."

A last sighing breath left her mouth. Serollyn fell onto her mother's lifeless body.

Marleon and Nestryn both bent to comfort Serollyn. "Your mother has found peace," Marleon told her, taking her into his arms.

"Has she?" Serollyn sobbed. "Or do the Death Stealers have her?"

*You were the Sneak's intended target,* Tolammy sent. *By giving her life for you, your mother defeated the Death Stealers.*

*The Sneak will not return.*

"Neither will my mother." Serollyn clung to Marleon, weeping. "I lost Krannel, and now I've lost her."

Abruptly she pushed herself free of Marleon's embrace and stood, wiping the tears from her face. "Mirivell!" she said. "What's happened to Mirivell? Did she die, too?" She gazed around, expecting the worst.

*I'm here.*

Serollyn looked for the source of the sending and saw Mirivell perched on the shoulder of the young guard who'd killed the messenger of death.

*Can you survive without my mother?*

*It is true that life-guides usually return to the Life Lenders along with their host,* Mirivell sent. *But the Life Lenders have allowed me to take a new host. Larkin is young and courageous, and the Life Lenders have gifted him with a life-guide.*

Larkin's face was filled with wonder. "I heard you," he said to Mirivell. "In my mind."

"All life-guides mindspeak," Nestryn told him. "And their hosts learn to do so, too. Lorry has."

Magistrate Pell came out from behind his desk. He ordered the guards to take Jode into custody and to remove San's body and take it to the mortuary. They hurried to obey.

Marleon wanted to know what a mortuary was.

"A place where bodies are prepared for burial," the magistrate said. He placed his hand on Serollyn's arm. "I am deeply sorry for your mother's death," he said. "Shall I have her body taken to the mortuary as well?"

Serollyn shook her head. "I want to wash her, dress her, and care for her in the manner of our people. We will take her body with us for burial on our way home.

"I had hoped that you would stay here and teach us more about life-guides," the magistrate said.

"You don't need us for that," Serollyn replied. "Lorry can help you, and so can Larkin."

But Nestryn said, "Larkin has only just received a life-guide, and Lorry has had little training. Tolammy and I will remain here. Lorry can reopen the Life Lenders' sanctuary, and those who wish to learn of the life-guides can come there, and I will teach them."

"But our own people need teaching," Marleon objected. Too many of them have lied about having life-guides."

"That is your job and Serollyn's," Nestryn said. "And I don't envy you the task. It may prove more difficult than mine."

## 24

# RETURN

Knowing they would fear the return trek through the forest, Serollyn assumed Dedryc and Feryn would choose to stay with Nestryn. But despite that fear, they both insisted in going with her and Marleon. Vali, too, declared herself ready to go home.

Nestryn and Tolammy, along with Larkin and Mirivell, Lorry and Glimmer, went with them for a short distance to help carry Joxlyn's body and to participate in the farewell ceremony.

They stopped in a clearing a half-day's trip into the forst. There they held vigil for Joxlyn and arranges a resting place for her beneath the forest trees. Covered with leaves and branches and bedecked with what wild flowers they could find in the underbrush, her body would lie there until consumed by insects and animals and thus returned to replenish the land and its creatures.

Serollyn sang the farewell songs, and she, Nestryn, and Marleon danced the intricate chain dance, using chains Vali fashioned from vines. The dance symbolized both the continuity of all life and the beginning and ending of an individual life, "nourished by the lives of others, and now given to nourish others' lives," as the final prayer concluded. The familiar ceremony eased Serollyn's grief, leaving only a dull ache. With the vigil and ceremonies completed, she had to say goodbye to Nestryn and Tollamy and also to her new friends.

Before they left, Larkin returned to Marleon his belt with the knife in its sheath and the bag of flints still hanging from it. He woud have returned the pistol as well, but Marleon refused it, saying, "I want no more of those death-dealing things. I'll do my hunting clan-style, with a spear or bow and arrows."

Serollyn, Marleon, Vali, Dedryc, and Feryn, went on through the deep forest with Delk as the only life-guide to protect them and show them the way.

Serollyn should have been glad for Vali's company, but despite her change of heart, Vali was not much help either with the routine of setting up nightly camps and keeping watch or with looking after Dedryc and Feryn. Fortunately the boys required far less looking after than they had previously. They seemed to be maturing at last. They even took turns at keeping watch at night and at helping prepare food.

They had little need to stop to hunt or fish on the return journey. Magistrate Pell had loaded them down with supplies, including a generous stock of vegetables and dried meat.

"What do you think my mother meant when she said she was proud to die for me and for my life-guide?" Serrolyn asked Marleon one day as they walked along a path they recognized as one used by their clan hunters. Their long trek was nearing its end. "Mother knew I didn't have a life-guide. I thought maybe Mirivell … But Mirivell went to Larkin."

With a puzzled frown Marleon shook his head, but Delk sent, *I think she meant that she exchanged her life for his.*

"I don't understand."

*Think about it,* Delk sent. *And look beside you.*

She looked on either side of her, seeing nothing and wondering what Delk was talking about. Then, as they passed through a patch of sunlight, a faint yellow blur moved along with her.

*Krannel?* She stared at what looked to her like a hazy yellow mist and saw two brown orbs meet her gaze.

*Krannel! You are back!*

"What are you talking about?" Vali asked.

"Don't you see him? There, he's coming clearer!"

"I see nothing," Vali declared.

"Neither do I," Marleon said. "But I guess Delk did."

*I am here,* came Krannel's familiar voice in her mind. And the yellow blur resolved into his beloved features, the black-tipped tail wagging, the black-tipped ears erect.

Serollyn hugged Krannel and scratched his ears and laughed at his wagging tail. "But why can't the others see you?" she asked.

*For now I am like other life-guides, visible only to the one to whom I am sent,* came his response.

"But I still see their life-guides."

*I gave you that gift. None can take it from you.*

"Couldn't Delk give *me* that gift?" Marleon asked. "I saw Mirivell and Glimmer and Tolammy when they showed themselves to the magistrate and to Larkin and the other guards. But that was for such a short time."

*And it was by their power, because they willed it,* Delk sent. *And because you wanted and needed to see them. I had nothing to do with it.*

"But couldn't you let me see all life-guides, the way Serollyn does?"

*When you need that gift, you will have it. But you may see Krannel now.*

Marleon gave a low whistle and bent to scratch Krannel's head. "I don't know how you came back, but I'm so glad to see you—really see you! I think I missed you almost as much as Serollyn did."

"Is it really Krannel?" Feryn asked. "I want to see him. I need to know I didn't kill him for good."

Thinking of how she'd helped Vali and the guards see the other life-guides, Serollyn placed Feryn's hand on Krannel's head.

Feryn's mouth formed an O. He dropped to his knees and hugged the dog, laying his head against Krannel's side.

"I want to see him, too," Dedryc begged.

She guided his hand to Krannel's nose and let Dedryc rub it. "I feel him," he said. "I can't see him, though."

"Maybe you're trying too hard," Serollyn suggested gently. "Just relax and pat his nose. And picture him the way you remember him."

"I see him! Not very well, but I do see him!" Dedryc's face glowed with happiness.

"Do you see him?" Serollyn dared to ask Vali.

"Faintly, yes, I think I do," Vali said.

"Do you think Feryn and I will get life-guides one day?" Dedryc asked them.

"I can't say," Serollyn replied. "It's possible that you will, but that's in the hands of the Life Lenders."

"The fact that you can see the life-guides now makes me feel that you will," Marleon offered.

"Hope so," Feryn said. "I'd like a springer. They're such fun to watch."

Serollyn gave him a hug. "A springer would be a good match for you," she said. "But we don't get to choose our life-guides. They choose us."

She saw the sadness that came over Vali's face and knew how much it hurt Vali to be without a life-guide and to have to return to the clan and have her deception exposed. That Vali had been willing to do so brought hope to Serollyn that her friend might someday receive a true life-guide. But she did not voice that hope, not wanting Vali to count on something that might never occur.

They made good progress on their way after that, Krannel gamboling along beside Serollyn and Delk padding silently next to Marleon.

Two days later, just past midday, they left the forest and passed through fields where men and women of their village were harvesting crops. They must have been an imposing sight: Serollyn and Marleon striding along together, with Delk at Marleon's side, Dedryc and Feryn marching along behind them, with Vali between them. Many workers stopped their toil to gawk.

In the village they split up, Serollyn going to find Sudy while Marleon headed for his parents' home and Vali went to hers. Dedryc and Feryn stayed with Serollyn.

Sudy was not at home. Serollyn went to the communal kitchen, where she was sure she'd find Sudy, along with many other older women, busy with preparations for the evening meal. Dedryc and Feryn hung back, too shy to go inside. She let them wait while she entered.

"Grandmother, I'm back," she called. "Back from the far side of the forest."

Sudy came and threw her arms around her.

"Grandmother, we've been to the far side of the forest, and I have so much to tell you about it."

"Not here," her grandmother cautioned.

The other women stared at her, faces dark with anger. One brandished a stirring spoon and scolded, "How dare you bring that dog in here! Have you learned nothing while you were gone?"

"Dog?" Serollyn laughed aloud. *They see you, Krannel? You're visible again? To everybody?*

*The Life Lenders have made it so. But do not laugh. It will cause a terrible division, and you must heal it.*

The dark looks and the shouts of "Get out! Go back where you came from!" emphasized his warning. Those shouters were mainly women who had no life-guides, but this was not the time to expose them. She persuaded Sudy to leave her work and return home, where they could talk.

She collected Dedryc and Feryn and introduced them to Sudy. Her grandmother hugged them and said, "You did right to bring the boys here."

They hurried to Sudy's cottage. Sudy ladled bowls of fish chowder from her ever-present pot and settled the boys at the table to eat while she and Serollyn talked.

Serollyn gave her grandmother a brief account of all that had happened, saving details for later. Sudy both rejoiced at and was saddened by the news of Joxlyn, and they were consoling each other when Marleon burst in.

"My grandfather, Old Morkle, he's killed himself," he cried. "Threw himself off the cliff west of the village."

"Oh, Marleon!" Serollyn embraced him. "Was it because he thought we'd expose his lie now that we've come back?"

"No, child, I doubt he knew you'd returned," Sudy said. "He's been consumed by guilt since you left. Just a couple of days ago he confessed to the clan that he lied all these years about having a life-guide and swore that others have done the same."

"So people know the truth?" Serollyn asked.

"Some believe what he said, and others say he was just a crazy old man," Sudy answered. "Now that you've arrived, things will be settled one way or another."

"So they still want to kill us," Serollyn said.

"Some do, but many will defend you."

"And I have Delk to protect me," Marleon said proudly.

Feryn and Dedryc rose, and Dedryc came to cling fearfully to Serollyn. Feryn, on the other hand, ran from the hut yelling, "I'm going to go get my springer."

Marleon started after him, but Sudy called him back. "No one will hurt him," she said. "No one knows him. And I suspect his life-guide may have summoned him."

Serollyn started to object that Feryn had no life-guide, only a dream of finding one some day. But Delk growled, and Krannel put his mouth over her hand and tugged gently with his teeth.

"Come outside," someone called. Serollyn recognized the imperious voice of the clan mother.

"We'd better go," Sudy advised.

They stepped out into the bright sunshine. A large number of clan members clustered there, the clan mother in the lead.

A second group stood to one side, watching, their faces grim. Serollyn's brother Corlon and his wife Laki led that group.

"You and your animals are not welcome here," the clan mother said, practically spitting the word "animals."

"We and our life-guides have returned to help our people, not bring trouble to them," Serollyn responded.

"We need no help from you," the clan mother said.

"Are you afraid that we will expose the fact that you have no life-guide? That your 'golden phoenix' is a lie?"

At Serollyn's audacious challenge, gasps and angry shouts broke out among the clan mother's followers. Corlon and Laki led their group nearer Serollyn.

"You can see my life-guide, but you refuse to believe that he is a life-guide," Serollyn said. "But can you doubt that Marleon's great-cat is his life-guide? Have you ever heard of a tame great-cat?"

She read doubt on some faces at that, but the clan mother shouted, "Life-guides cannot be seen. You and Marleon are nothing but heretics and troublemakers. Leave or be punished, possibly with death."

"We've only just come back," Serollyn said. "We will not leave. We haven't come to make trouble. You fear us because of what we know, but we can't help that."

Someone picked up a handful of pebbles from the path and hurled them at Serollyn and Marleon. Only a few found a mark, and they merely stung. But larger stones lined the path, and one or two people picked them up.

"Where is the chief elder?" Sudy called out. "If this is an authorized clan meeting, he should be here."

That made a few people pause. The chief elder was not present. But most ignored Sudy's objection. A large stone flew past her shoulder. Another landed at Serollyn's feet. Marleon's sharp outcry told Serollyn that a third had found its mark.

"Since when do those who follow the Life Lenders do the Death Stealers' work?" Serollyn shouted.

That brought a lull in the stone throwing, but only until the clan mother called out, "The Life Lenders reject those who bring discord to the clan. Your lives belong to the Death Stealers and deserve to be taken by them."

With that, the clan mother herself stooped, picked up a stone, and hurled it toward Serollyn. It fell short of its mark, but a younger man threw one with better aim. It hit Serollyn on the cheek, stunning her briefly and opening a gash.

Shouting, "Stop!" her brother Corlon made his way to Serollyn. Serollyn saw his orsa lumbering along beside him. "I'm with you, and so are my friends," he said. "But there aren't enough of us to prevail."

A large stone flew toward him. The orsa deflected it with a swipe of its large paw. But the stones were coming faster now, and the life-guides could stop only a few.

"Your orsa," Serollyn said to Corlon. "I must touch him."

"Bors?" Corlon asked, dodging a stone.

*I hear. I understand what she wishes.* The shaggy creature shambled to Serollyn's side, and she placed a hand on his rough fur and her other hand on Krannel. "Marleon, take my arm," she said, "and place your other hand on Delk's head."

There was no time to explain what she was doing, but Marleon followed her instructions without question, and Sudy seemed to need no explanation. She lifted Jec and placed him on Serollyn's shoulder, keeping one hand on him.

Serollyn was trying to recreate the force that had

allowed Larkin and the other guards to see the life-guides. But they had wanted to see them; these people did not. And they couldn't maintain the necessary contact while dodging stones.

But then a child's voice cried out, "Look! Look! I see father's orsa." It was Corlon and Laki's young son, Vannon. He broke away from Laki and ran to his father.

"Don't hurt my child," Corlon shouted.

Children were precious to the clan. Several people dropped the stones they were about to throw. Only a few ventured to hurl more stones, and those stones fell short of their mark, perhaps indicating diminished enthusiasm for the persecution.

"I see Bors," Vannon exclaimed again. "May I pet him, please?"

"You may touch him," Corlon said with a proud smile.

Dedryc peered out from behind Sudy. "Feryn's coming," he announced. "With his springer!"

Feryn ran toward them, a springer bobbing up and down beside him. He skirted the hostile crowd and approached from the side where Corlon's wife and friends stood. They quickly parted to let him pass.

"His name is Leeper," Feryn said breathlessly.

Dedryc came from behind Sudy and reached out to touch the springer. "Hello, Leeper," he said. A surprised smile lit his face. "He spoke to me. I heard him in my mind."

Serollyn had heard him, too. The new life-guide said, *Hello, Dedryc. Thank you for letting Feryn come to find me. I am sent to you both.*

Serollyn had never heard of two people sharing a life-guide, but the twins were so close that it seemed right.

Other children among Corlon's friends shouted and jumped around in excitement. Their excitement spread to the clan mother's group. There were few children among that group, but those few saw what the adults did not. Eagerly they pointed out to one another and to their parents this life-guide and that, the accuracy of their observations leaving little doubt that they truly saw what they claimed.

Some of the children ran forward and, showing no fear of Delk, patted him and Leeper before their anxious parents could intervene.

The parents came close to drag the children away but stayed, staring in wonder, as they, too, saw the life-guides. Clan members cried out in awe and admiration.

Then there were shouts of anger, no longer directed at Serollyn and her friends but at those with no life-guides.

Chief among those was the clan mother. Soon everyone was demanding, "Where is your golden phoenix? Show him to us."

The clan mother tried to protest that the bird had merely flown into the trees for a time, but that was so clearly a lie that all those around her jeered and hissed.

"Stop," Sudy called out. "Listen!"

With effort she got their attention.

"The Life Lenders send the life-guides to unite us, not to divide us," Sudy said. "Those who do not have life-guides may yet receive them, but if they don't, they are no less a part of our clan. Let this day be one of rejoicing in this marvelous gift. You have been allowed to see the life-guides, I believe, because of the courage and faith of these young people. Now we must show our courage and faith by putting aside anger and thoughts of retribution and joining together to give thanks to the Life Lenders."

"You shall lead us, Sudy," someone called, and others took up the cry.

"Let Sudy be clan mother," the piper shouted, his gazelle prancing along with him as he strode to the front of the crowd. "My pipes will summon all those not already gathered here, and we will give thanks, as you say. But you take the part of clan mother and lead the prayers and the songs."

Everyone applauded that idea. Serollyn hugged her grandmother. "Do it," she urged. "Our clan mother must have a life-guide."

From somewhere the chief elder had come to join the group. He added his voice to the piper's, and Sudy could not refuse.

Feryn and Dedryc scarcely seemed to notice the commotion around them, being too occupied with hugging and mindspeaking with their life-guide.

Serollyn nudged Marleon and spoke in his ear, "We won't need to worry about those two any more. With a life-guide, they'll be accepted into the clan."

Marleon put his arm around her. "This is truly a great day," he said. "Your mother would be so proud of you."

"Of us all," Serollyn said, resting her head on his shoulder.

*She is here, and she is proud,* Krannel said. *It was her spirit uniting with mine and with Delk's, yes, and with Leeper's, that let us reveal all the other life-guides, first to the children, and then, on the strength of the children's belief, to the adults.*

"Will the life-guides remain visible to everyone?" Serollyn asked.

*That depends on you and your people,* Delk sent. *You must help them remember the worth of all life. That is not an easy lesson, but you and Marleon have been entrusted with the task of teaching it. Your work will be difficult, but you will have the aid of all life-guides.*

Marleon looked at Serollyn. "With that help, we can't fail, can we?"

# THE END

# ABOUT THE AUTHOR

Elenora Rose Sabin writes as E. Rose Sabin simply because people have so much difficulty spelling and pronouncing her first name. Rose is easier.

Ms. Sabin taught Spanish and language arts to middle school students for many years before turning to a career as a novelist. She writes what she enjoys reading: science fiction and fantasy novels. She has written novels for adults and teens and has recently published a children's chapter book.

A dog lover, Ms. Sabin has two rescue dogs to keep her entertained and distracted. They make certain that she takes breaks from sitting at the computer to play with them and to let them in and out of the house to romp in the back yard.

She enjoys hearing from readers, who can post messages on her Facebook author page: E. Rose Sabin's Books. She hopes readers will also check out her web site: www.erosesabin.com

# BOOKS BY E. ROSE SABIN

## THE ARUCADI BOOKS:

### ARUCADI: THE BEGINNING

> MISTRESS OF THE WIND
> BRINGERS OF MAGIC
> A MIX OF MAGICS

### ARUCADI: SCHOOL SERIES

> A PERILOUS POWER
> A SCHOOL FOR SORCERY
> WHEN THE BEAST RAVENS

### TRAVELS THROUGH ARUCADI:

> BRYTE'S ASCENT

## THE TERRANO TRILOGY:

> SHADOW OF A DEMON
> THE GIFT OF THE TRINDE TREE
> TOUCH OF DEATH

SEDUCTION OF THE SCEPTER

WERE HOUSE

GRANDY'S GRAND INVENTIONS (A Children's Chapter Book)

TO THE FAR SIDE OF THE FOREST (For Teens)

## COMING SOON:

> DEATHRIGHT

# ACKNOWLEDGMENTS

I want to thank the many people who read or heard me read all or parts of this book and were kind enough to offer constructive criticism and to point out errors. First of these is my critiquing partner, author Diane Sawyer, whose sharp eye caught many errors and whose careful reading brought valuable suggestions for improvement. Writer Marylou Hess graciously consented to read and critique the manuscript, and pointed out problems neither I nor Diane had caught. Joyce Levesque has long been a faithful reader and critiquer of all my manuscripts, and is always helpful and encouraging. The members of the St. Petersburg Writers Club offered invaluable advice both on the manuscript and on the cover art. Teddy, a seventh grader, volunteered to read the manuscript and offer his opinion as a member of the target age group for the novel. His enthusiastic response was deeply gratifying. It is interesting to note that each reader spotted different ways in which the story could be improved, a fact which points out the importance of having several readers review a manuscript before it's sent out to a publisher.

I used the digital art program DAZ3D to produce the cover art. It is a complex program, one I am still learning, and I would never have succeeded without the help and encouragement of artist Rubey Shea, who spent a great deal of time teaching me the technical aspects of the program. It still did not come easily for me, and I often availed myself of the DAZ help desk and of one patient and understanding service representative in particular. Thank you, Topher Spencer!

I'm sure I've omitted others who should be acknowledged for their help and their encouragement, but the omission is not intentional. There have simply been too many to recall them all. I began work on this novel many years ago, set it aside for a long while because I wasn't satisfied with it, and went back to it as I gained experience and felt I could fix its faults. Whether I succeeded or not my readers will have to judge. I'm sure you will discover problems I have overlooked or things you wish I had done differently. Despite the help of the readers I have named or forgotten to name, I find needed changes every time I read through the manuscript. The fault is not theirs but mine. But there comes a time to declare it finished and send it off to make its way in the world.

Reader, be gentle. And please feel free to leave any comments you have on my Facebook author's page: http://www.facebook.com/erosesabinsbooks.

www.ingramcontent.com/pod-product-compliance
Lightning Source LLC
Chambersburg PA
CBHW070609130626
46556CB00001B/314